THE BARS THAT HOLD ME

ED GRACE

ALSO BY ED GRACE

Titles in the Jay Sullivan Series

Assassin Down

Kill Them Quickly

The Bars That Hold Me

A Deadly Weapon

The End of a Life (Novella)

Copyright © 2020 by Rick Wood / Ed Grace

All rights reserved.

No part of this book may be reproduced in any form or by any electronic or mechanical means, including information storage and retrieval systems, without written permission from the author, except for the use of brief quotations in a book review.

LONDON HEATHROW AIRPORT

CHAPTER ONE

It was a late spring evening as the car drove through Tunnel Road East, onto Inner Ring E, and stopped in a drop off bay outside the entrance to Terminals 2 and 3.

Many people rushed past, pulling their luggage, dragging their kids; their haste more important than politeness.

None of them had any idea they were about to die.

Zain gazed out of the window; his chin rested on his fist. He watched a mother in a summery dress, her sunglasses perched on top of her forehead, holding hands with an excitable girl. It was not the time of year for sunglasses and summery dresses — but this was what holiday makers did. They wore clothes that matched where they were going, not where they were.

It occurred to Zain that this woman would never reach her destination. Neither would her daughter. She would perish in that dress.

"You're nervous," said Azeer, in the seat next to him.

Zain did not respond. He looked down, feeling a little ashamed.

"It's okay to be nervous," Azeer said. "You're about to do something incredible. You're bound to be excited."

Zain wasn't sure whether excited was the right word.

He turned to Azeer, who always seemed so confident. Azeer had personally overseen Zain's training before choosing him for the martyrdom program. It was an honour, and Zain should be proud.

He was proud.

He was, really.

He just wished he hadn't left things with his family the way he had. That he would go to Heaven with his family still grieving his decisions.

He told himself to stop fretting. To trust in Allah. To thank Allah for the honour. To thank Allah for guiding him to this moment, ensuring he had the strength, and would continue to have the strength for as long as he needed it.

Only, he didn't feel particularly strong.

He knew Heaven was waiting for him. He knew Allah was waiting for him. He knew that the rest of Alhami would celebrate his name, as would any true Islamist who believed the same as him — he would be a hero.

He just didn't feel much like one.

Azeer put his hand on Zain's shoulder, smiled, and spoke softly, "Allaha Akbar."

Zain nodded.

Azeer was right.

"Allaha Akbar," he repeated.

The man in the passenger seat — Zain didn't know his name; they weren't allowed to know the generals' names — passed the vest over.

It was black with rectangular objects attached to it. They looked like bricks with wires.

Azeer took off his top. Looked out of the window, checked for CCTV.

"We have parked away from the cameras," Azeer assured him. "We have planned this to every detail, so please, trust us."

Zain did trust them.

Really, he did.

He put the vest on. It was heavy. He wasn't sure how he was going to walk into the airport without being noticed. He put his t-shirt back on, and it looked thick and noticeable.

"Put a jacket on," Azeer said, handing him a hoodie.

Zain put it on. It covered it up a lot better. He just hoped no one looked at him for too long. He may be able to get away with a quick glance, but not a prolonged stare.

But then again, did it matter? He had bombs strapped to him. How would anyone stop him?

Azeer opened Zain's hand and placed the detonator in his palm. It was like a little radio, except it had a red button rather than a speaker.

It felt surreal. He'd been through so much training for this moment, so much preparation, so much planning, and now here he was, bomb vest on and the detonator in his hand.

Zain placed the detonator in his pocket.

Azeer grabbed Zain's hand and twisted it into a handshake. Azeer gripped firmly, and smiled determinedly.

"As-salamu 'alaykum," Azeer told him.

Peace be upon you.

"As-salamu 'alaykum," Zain said back.

He opened the car door.

Stepped out.

Looked at the busy entrance of the country's busiest airport. Considered the hundreds who were going to perish.

Then remembered why they must perish.

He opened the doors and walked inside.

LONDON, UNITED KINGDOM

THIRTY DAYS EARLIER

CHAPTER TWO

Once upon a time, Jay Sullivan had been a ruthless, expert assassin, as brilliant at his job as he was at being a father. People feared him, and he truly believed he was defending his country by killing those he was told to kill. He kept his daughter shielded and made sure she always felt loved. Now he was—

What? What was he now?

He had no idea what the end of that sentence was.

He was far from a good father, considering he had no idea where his daughter was. He didn't make people cower when he walked into a room. He definitely wasn't ruthless, or expert, or brilliant.

So what was he now?

He was damaged.

He bore a mark over his heart, indents in the back of his skull, and burns on his back — yet it was in his mind where the most damage had been done. This was where his thoughts bullied him, constantly, reminding him of the faces of those he'd murdered, the tears of those who'd witnessed, and the eyes of a daughter turned against him.

The memories that haunted him most were the hits he had performed for the Falcons. A secret government organisation who had trained and employed him, only to betray him.

At this particular moment, as he lay in bed, organising the ceiling tiles into sections without any conscious intention to do so, it was a moment of his training that his mind chose to torment him with.

Though training wasn't the right word. Training was something one went through to gain a qualification, or acquire a new skill, or learn how to cook. What Sullivan had gone through was so much more. It was indoctrination and reconditioning; a complete overhaul of every perception he had. On the good days, it was manipulation, and on the worst, it was torture.

"Your father was right to kill himself," he remembered his mentor, Alexander, saying. Sullivan had just turned eighteen, and it had only been weeks since he was recruited.

"What?" Inevitably, Sullivan had reacted aggressively. "Who the fuck are you—"

"This is what we do, Jay. We kill the weak. We kill the evil people. We keep the balance."

"He was—"

"Weak, Sullivan. He was weak."

"Fuck off, I—"

"You are not like your father."

This had stumped him. It was something he had longed to hear, but something no one had ever said. He hated the thought that he might end up like a father who had abused him, before killing his mother and turning the gun on himself. Sullivan had spent the next two years being kicked out of children's homes because of his anger, and he was worried he was turning out the same way — yet here, for the first time, was someone saying that he was not like his father at all.

And, because Alexander knew how much Sullivan wished to hear those words, it had been easy to manipulate Sullivan by saying it.

"Yes, Jay. You are not like him at all. He was an amateurish killer. You will be a magnificent master of death — it is what you were destined to be."

Sullivan sat up. Rubbed his eyes. He couldn't think about this any longer. It was making him crazy and he was desperate for a drink.

He looked to his right, where Kelly lay.

Beautiful. Intelligent. Perfect. Her gentle breathing pushed a strand of hair from over her face. How is it possible, he wondered, that someone can wake up from sleep looking so damn faultless?

He felt like shit. His stomach was acidic, his chin was stubbly, his throat was dry — and he was certain he looked awful. Yet, here she was, the epitome of perfection.

She'd told him she loved him.

He'd told her she didn't.

Again, he thought, how strange it is the situations we end up in. Memories of his torture disguised as training taunted him, and he resented his government for it — yet, beside him lay an agent from MI5; a woman who worked for the same government who had betrayed him and hunted him.

But it was not an issue. He did not ask her about what she did, and she never brought it up. She was too good for that. She would never be tempted to give up information.

He told her who he was a few days ago. She said she didn't care, so he'd told her more about what he'd been through, about how the government is probably hunting him, how he was betrayed by his country. At first, she was fine with it.

Then he mentioned that it was the Falcons he had worked for, and she'd replied stiffly, "You need to stop talking now."

He wondered if he'd fallen in love with her.

Hell, he wondered if a man like him was capable of love. How could someone who'd killed as many people as he had feel emotions in the same way ordinary people do?

Maybe he did love her, in his own fucked up kind of way.

But he'd stayed in her life for too long already. Bad things happened to people he cared about. Especially women.

Then again, she was both an MI5 agent and an ex-marine. She could handle herself.

But he had been the world's greatest assassin, and look what had happened to him.

He fumbled for pills in the pockets of his trousers left discarded on the floor. He took a few, and it quelled the pain in his chest. He had a heart condition, and it never gave up causing him pain at inopportune moments.

For a brief few seconds, he wondered where his daughter was at that moment; something that often crossed his mind. He'd lost Talia when she was in her early teens and, when he discovered her years later, his biggest fears had been realised — she had turned into a killer. Like him.

They had since gone their own ways; something he regretted every day.

Kelly's 6:00 a.m. alarm went off. She groaned, turned her body over and hit the off button. She rubbed her eyes, rolled onto her back, and looked up at Sullivan.

"Are you okay?" she asked. He realised she'd woken up to find him watching her.

"Yeah, sorry," he said, pushing himself out of bed. He searched for his clothes and quickly dressed himself.

"Do you want to get breakfast?" she asked, sitting up and checking her emails on her phone.

"No, I should be going."

"You should be going?"

"Mmhm."

"Where exactly is it you should be going?"

"Oh, you know, places."

"For a man who has no job and is on the run, you seem to have a very busy morning."

He stopped rushing. Leant against the windowsill. Watched her, wishing he wasn't so stupid; wishing he could stop being a fool and just spend some time with her before she went to work.

"This is London," she said. "There's a diner around the corner where you won't be recognised."

"Recognised? In London? There are so many people in this city I doubt they'd recognise Bin Laden if he went walking around the market."

"Bin Laden? You do know the Americans caught him, right?"

"I'm a little behind in the whole terrorist thing. Who are we even fighting at the moment?"

She laughed. "A lot of people."

She stepped out of bed. She slipped off her night dress and went to find some underwear, but stopped as she noticed Sullivan staring at her naked body.

"You know, we don't have to go out for breakfast...."

Sullivan really needed to be going. The longer he spent with someone, the more danger they were in.

Fuck it, he thought. *She's a big girl.*

He stepped forward, slid his arms around her waist, and pressed his lips against hers. They never did end up having breakfast.

CHAPTER THREE

Umar stood in the centre of the empty room with Naji to his right, and his father to his left. The room itself was once a tattoo parlour, and had been bought by their leader, Azeer Nadeem, for what HM Revenue and Customs were informed would soon be a taxi rank.

Azeer had no intention of it being a taxi rank.

It had been bought for this moment. So that, when the time came, Umar was only a few steps away from Camden Market. This gave them a chance to pray before his sacrifice.

Umar's father placed the bomb jacket on Umar. Umar stood still, his arms out, staring absently ahead as his father tightened the straps and placed Umar's coat over it. The vest looked thick, almost too big, but it didn't matter — it would be less than a minute after leaving this room before he hit the detonator. If anyone had any suspicions, there would be no time to do anything about it.

"Are you okay?" his father asked.

Naji sneered at them for speaking English. He only spoke Arabic. But Umar was brought up in England, he was educated here — it was the language he understood the best.

Besides, this was not a moment for Alhami. This was a moment for Umar and his father. A touching moment — the moment Umar had waited his whole life for.

"I am proud of you," his father said. "So very, very proud."

Umar had craved those words for so long. He'd waited for this moment for longer than he'd ever admitted, and he was grateful.

"You are ready," his father said, and they prepared themselves for prayer.

Umar washed his right hand three times, and his left hand three times. As he waited for the other two, he turned toward the South East, the direction of Makkah, and tried to avoid letting his mind wander. He'd just end up thinking about what he was about to do. He didn't want to admit to the others that he was scared. He already knew what they would tell him — that a glorious afterlife awaited him; a wondrous reward for his sacrifice. He was to be a hero, and would be celebrated as such.

The others joined his side, and they began their prayer.

"Allahu Akbar," they said.

He placed his right hand on top of his left and looked to the ground, almost in perfect unison to the other two.

"Subhanaka allahumma wa bi hamdika wa tabara kasmuka wa ta'ala jadduka wa la ilaha ghariuku."

He took in a deep breath, held it, and let it out — but he did so silently. He did not want anyone to see his nerves, nor his trepidation. He wanted them to see his strength — unfortunately, he had little of that to show.

"A'udhu billahi minash shaitanir rajim."

Azeer had told him this was a great honour.

"Bismillahir rahmanir rahim."

They bent over, saying, "Allahu Akbar," then placed their hands on their knees.

"Subhana Rabbiyal Adhiim."

He rarely said this in Arabic, but Naji had insisted. The prayers were supposed to give him the strength he needed, but he gained little of it by speaking in a language he had only recently learnt.

He decided to say the words in Arabic, but think them in English.

Allah hears those who praise him. Glory be to Allah.

It was true; Allah would hear the ones who praise him.

It was in Allah's glory Umar was about to act.

And, with the moment of self-belief he had been desiring, he was ready.

He hoped his father would be just as proud after he was gone.

He hoped they all would be.

CHAPTER FOUR

Sullivan walked leisurely through Camden Market. He so rarely had a chance to walk slowly and without purpose. He usually ensured he didn't spend too much time in one place, but he was beginning to feel settled. Kelly's company, as much as he denied it, was growing on him.

Which was only going to make it harder when he did leave. He could not afford to be complacent, just as he could not afford to fall in love.

But, as he enjoyed the warmth of a hot summer's day, he allowed himself to feel what he so rarely felt — contentedness.

A moment when he was okay with being okay.

He passed *Market Hall*, the indoor part of the market. He wanted to enjoy the sunny weather, so wandered aimlessly around a few of the stalls outside. He stopped at a clothes stall and perused a few items with no intention of buying anything. He had enough money left over from his days as an assassin to afford the best suits anyone could wear, but it was still nice to stop, look, and pretend to be like everyone else.

A man to his left lifted a few polo shirts to find one in

blue. A woman across from Sullivan helped her husband pick a jacket, holding them against his frame. A child tried on a coat.

Such small, uncelebrated moments that these people took for granted. They were the kind of moments Sullivan could never have.

He resented Alexander and the Falcons, not just for the lives they forced him to take, but for the life they had taken from him. Sure, the angry eighteen-year-old version of himself may well have ended up in prison, but it would have been his choice. And he would not have been coerced into killing people.

He shook his head. Why was he thinking about this again?

He wished he could think about something else, but this was what his mind did; replayed the worst parts of his history over and over. He tried to occupy his thoughts as much as he could, as any moment of inactivity was a moment where his mind would present the bloodied face of a man he'd killed, or the bashed-in skull of a target, or the horrified faces of a family witnessing the death of a loved one.

The reminder was always there.

Always.

"Hey, Mister," said a curious voice from behind Sullivan.

He turned around to see a young boy, maybe ten or eleven, wearing a taqiyya — a white cap as worn by Muslim men — staring at him.

"Hello," said Sullivan.

"You look really angry."

"I do?"

"Yes. Your face was twisting, like this."

The boy's face twisted, his lips pouting and his features squeezing, and Sullivan couldn't help but laugh. Perhaps his thoughts were seeping through to his facial expression more than he was aware.

"Wow," Sullivan said. "Is that really what I look like?"

"It was. You're smiling now."

"Oh, that's good."

"Do you want some lunch?"

"Excuse me?"

"My dad said not to do this, but he has a stall over there, and nobody's buying anything. I just thought, maybe you'd like some lunch."

"What's he serving?"

"Curry. He's got lots of kinds. It's not expensive."

Sullivan wanted to say, *it is half eleven in the morning, I imagine not many people are wanting curry yet* — but didn't.

"I would love some curry," he said, instead.

"Okay, it's this way," the boy said, rushing through the crowd, Sullivan trying to keep up. "I'm Sajid by the way."

"It's nice to meet you, Sajid."

"What's your name?"

Sullivan hesitated. It was best that Sajid didn't know his name.

"Clint," he said instead. He used to love Dirty Harry films as a kid, and it was the first thing that came to his mind.

"That's a funny name."

"I guess it is."

He arrived at the stall where a fine assortment of curries were on display. Sullivan took a ten-pound note from his pocket and handed it over.

"I'll have a Jalfrezi, please," he said. The man served it up, and went to hand Sullivan five pounds in change, but Sullivan waved it away.

"Keep it," he said. He had millions in a bank, and this looked like good curry.

Sajid watched intently as Sullivan had his first taste.

"Beautiful," Sullivan declared. "Absolutely beautiful."

Sajid's face lit up. "I helped make that one!"

"You did a good job."

"Thank you!"

"I'm going to have a walk. It was nice to meet you, Sajid."

"You too, Clint."

Sullivan smiled and walked away. He wasn't lying, it was good curry. He didn't feel particularly hungry, but he ate it, if only for the pleasure it gave Sajid. Once he'd finished, he searched for a bin. He walked a little bit out of the market to find one, and placed his finished container inside.

Someone barged into him as he did, and quickly apologised without breaking their stride.

This man drew Sullivan's attention. Something wasn't right about him. He looked anxious, yet determined. He was striding toward Market Hall, wiping sweat from his brow. His coat was bulging. His top half was a lot thicker than his bottom half. Either he'd missed a lot of leg days in the gym, or...

Then Sullivan wondered... why was he wearing a coat? It was hot, so much so that a lot of men were walking around with no t-shirt on at all. No one in their right mind would go out in a coat. So what was he trying to cover up?

"Shit!"

The man paused outside *Market Hall*, looked inside, took a detonator from his pocket, and ran into the building.

"Everyone get down!" Sullivan shouted, and every face turned to look at him. "Everyone get down, bomb!"

Initially, people looked at him like he was mad, but the word *bomb* made people listen. It still made little difference, as *Market Hall* was where the man had gone. How on earth was Sullivan meant to go in there and evacuate people without being caught in the blast himself?

He just had to save those he could.

"Everyone get away from the building!" he shouted.

He was about to retreat himself, until he saw Sajid. Just outside *Market Hall*. Wandering absentmindedly into the building.

"Sajid, no!" Sullivan screamed.

Without another thought, he sprinted toward the building.

Sajid paused, turned, and looked at Sullivan.

With an expression of confused playfulness, Sajid smiled and waved.

"Get back!" Sullivan shouted.

Sajid looked back, confused, cupping his ear as if to tell Sullivan to speak up.

"I said, get back! It's about to—"

The explosion engulfed Market Hall in flames, and sent Sullivan flying into a nearby stall.

CHAPTER FIVE

Sullivan opened his eyes seconds later and tried to ignore the ringing in his ears.

He rolled over, struggled to his feet, and limped forward, coughing on the smoke; it was so thick he could barely see.

He lifted his t-shirt and covered his mouth, waving black clouds out of his eyes, hobbling forward. There was an ache in his leg, and a wheeze in his breath — but he had suffered such injuries before.

At first, there was a silence; sickening, unbearable silence. A rumble had preceded the deafening roar of the explosion, but for a moment after the impact, everything was numb.

Then the screaming began. Not from inside the building — all that came from *Market Hall* was smoke and fire; the screams came from the people outside it. People Sullivan couldn't see through the clouds of grey and black.

He forced himself forward, not entirely sure what he was doing. Did he really think he could help these people? They were either dead, or dying. He was trained in killing, not bringing people back to life.

Nevertheless, he persevered. The ringing in his ears lessened, and the screaming grew louder.

The first body he came to was barely recognisable. Half of the face was intact, but the rest was covered in burns. A woman, in desperate denial, sat over the body, shaking it. Sullivan thought about helping, but the man was dead.

He struggled forward until he reached the doors to *Market Hall*, and shielded his face from the heat of the flames. A few burnt bodies had been thrown from the building and lay outside the entrance. He could do nothing but check to see if any of them were still alive.

He passed the first one, who was an old man, burns covering his empty face.

The next was a woman, possibly in her thirties. He put a hand on her throat. No pulse. She was holding a blanket, but the blanket was empty.

Across from her was a battered and broken pram, covered in ash.

Across from that was her baby.

He kept walking, stepping over bodies, glancing to see if there was anyone who he could help, but all he found was death.

Sirens rang out in the distance.

He crouched, keeping low, where the smoke was less thick, trying to see the bodies more clearly. With each dead face he saw, his mind plunged its fist into the depths of his memory and pulled out the face of a corpse he'd once created. Every child, every mother, and every father he came across conjured another piece of trauma he'd so poorly repressed.

He stumbled into the body of a boy and reluctantly looked upon the corpse's face. It didn't register at first, then in an abrupt hit of shock, he recognised the childish features that remained so still.

"Sajid..."

Sullivan knew he was dead, but it didn't matter. He insisted to himself that there was still a chance, that Sajid could still be revived, and he placed his mouth over the boy's, breathed out, not just once, but again, and again, and again.

He interlocked his fingers and pumped on Sajid's heart.

He breathed into his mouth, then pumped the chest. Breathed out, then pumped.

Sajid wasn't moving.

And, not so much in a decisive moment, but in a wave of overwhelming sadness, Sullivan understood that Sajid wasn't going to move again.

The boy had probably died upon impact. If not, then the fall on his head could have killed him, or the burns on his body.

Oh, God, Sullivan hadn't even noticed the burns on his body. Sajid's death would have been terrifying, and he would have suffered.

He saw his daughter in Sajid's face. Despite many differences between them, he suddenly thought about what it would be like to hold Talia like this. What it would be like to see her die.

Sajid was someone's child too.

Sullivan fell onto his back, and he didn't move.

He laid beside Sajid, making sure the boy wasn't alone, making sure that Sajid did not have to experience the kind of solitude he subjected himself to.

The sirens grew louder. There were lots of them now. People started running in.

One fireman tried to see if he was alive, and he batted their hands away, told them he was fine and to go check on others.

Sullivan tried not to care about the bodies that surrounded him. It was easier that way.

He remained still, lying on the blood-soaked street, feeling the heat of nearby fire, not moving.

He stayed with Sajid until his body was collected.

CHAPTER SIX

Kelly stood with her colleague, Henry Jameson, watching the news, just as aghast as everyone else at MI5.

The room was in a commotion, people rushing from seats, bashing keys at their computer, shouting, demanding, asking — but Kelly and Jameson, the two people responsible for leading counterterrorism operations, could only stand still in disbelief that they had not caught this before it happened.

"We are hearing that the attack happened at Camden Market, about half an hour ago, believed to have been carried out by a suicide bomber. We aren't sure of the number of casualties yet, but all we can see are the fire and police officers pulling out dead bodies."

The news did not tell them anything they didn't already know. Islamic extremist. Suicide bomber. Many dead.

"Has anyone claimed responsibility yet?" Jameson asked one of his subordinates.

"Not heard anything," the man said, dashing past, adding, "sorry, I have to get this done for Maya."

Everyone in their team was working as they should, and

they did not need further instructions, so Kelly and Jameson retreated to their office at the back of the room.

They sat in silence, but neither sat still; shifting in their seat, fidgeting with their hands, glancing out of the window and at framed pictures of their family.

Kelly knew that they needed to start acting, that they had to lead, that they needed to get involved and find out what their team knew.

The shock was just taking a while to sink in.

"How the fuck—" Jameson went to say, then stopped.

"I—" Kelly went to respond, but found herself equally perplexed.

She stood, unable to sit still any longer.

"We need to do something," she said. "We can't sit in here any longer."

"I know, I just — how did this get past us?"

"We won't find that out sitting in here."

"Everyone's doing what they are supposed to do. We can't instruct them until we have their intel. Just let them work for another ten minutes, then let's see what they have."

"You're right, I just think we should show our faces. Hiding in our office doesn't look good."

"We are not hiding. Far as they are concerned, we are talking strategy."

"And what is our strategy, Henry? How the hell did we not see this?"

"I don't even—"

A knock on the office door silenced them.

"Come in," Jameson said, and a man entered, a bit scruffy and dishevelled. He was one of the guys who worked on network monitoring. Toby, or something.

"What?" Jameson barked.

"You might want to see this."

"What is it?" Kelly asked.

"A video claiming responsibility."

"Is it credible?"

"Think so."

Kelly and Henry rushed from the office, trailing Toby through to the next room, where a video was projected onto the screen.

A man, with his face disguised and wearing a thawb — an ankle-length, tunic-like garment — stood in the centre of what appeared to be a cave, though Kelly knew that didn't mean much. The setting would be deliberate, probably to make them think they were hiding out somewhere. Chances are, this was done in their basement.

"Play it," she instructed.

Toby hit the space bar and the video began.

"I am speaking on behalf of Alhami, in Allah's name."

Kelly bowed her head.

Alhami. Named as such because it means The Protector. They were a terrorist cell of Islamic extremists they had been tracking for a while, but hadn't taken as seriously as other terrorists they'd chosen to prioritise — Alhami had never committed an attack, and didn't appear to have the resources to do something on this scale. All they had ever done was rant about the West and how infidels should die.

"By now I hope you see that we are serious. By now, I hope you understand that we are prepared to commit unrelenting blows upon our enemies in the West. Because of the detainment of our Muslim brothers in the United Kingdom, we are focusing our demonstrations on you. And this is not the last."

"Detainment of Muslim brothers?" Kelly said to Jameson. "Do you think he means Azeer Nadeem?"

"Definitely," Jameson said.

If that was the case, then this was only going to get worse. They suspected Azeer Nadeem of being the leader of Alhami, but had felt safe in the knowledge that he was currently serving twelve years for attempted murder. Azeer had claimed he'd stabbed a man while defending himself during a racist attack, and the Muslim community was livid when he had been sentenced to prison. No wonder they were stepping up their aggression.

"You attack us, and you hold our brothers for defending our rights, then we will attack you for denying those rights. I hope, from today's attack, that you understand how serious we are."

"Could Azeer be running this from the inside?" Jameson quickly suggested.

"No idea."

"Should we caution and interview him?"

"And give away that we know who he is?"

They turned their attention back to the screen.

"And so, to the people of the United Kingdom, we say this — you are not safe. This was only the beginning. You can expect two more attacks in the next thirty days. Each attack will be bigger than the last, and you can expect more of your people to die."

Despite the man's face being concealed, they could still see a grin widening. He added, "Allahu akbar," then the video ended.

Everyone's face turned to Kelly and Jameson, who stared at the video in disbelief.

More attacks? Bigger than the last?

"What do we do?" asked Toby.

Kelly felt her phone ringing. That's when she remembered — Sullivan was going to Camden Market that morning.

Jameson immediately began issuing instructions as Kelly rushed into the office.

CHAPTER SEVEN

Sullivan trudged away from the smoke until he reached the police tape. Crowds were gathering, full of people standing in stunned silence. Some with their arms around each other. Others in isolation.

Fire officers ran in and out, some tackling the remaining flames, some helping to transport bodies.

Reporters were already here, standing in front of their cameras with the devastating scene behind them. It made Sullivan feel sick. To them, this was a good shot. To them, this was an opportunity to further their career. To them — this was something they were pleased they got to first, so they could get the scoop.

One reporter ran up to Sullivan as he emerged, grabbing his arm.

"Hello, are you okay?" she asked, the camera pointing at him.

"Get that damn camera out of my face."

"Were you in the attack? Did you see what happened? Are you—"

Sullivan grabbed the camera and threw it to the floor, smashing the lens.

"What the fuck?" the cameraman said.

Sullivan grabbed hold of the man's collar and pulled his face within inches of his own.

Not only did he not want to be recognised, he also did not want some bastard shoving a camera in his face and asking questions.

The man quickly became apologetic, fearing an imminent beating.

Sullivan let him go and wandered onward. He passed weeping onlookers. People were showing up and demanding to know if their loved ones were found, and police officers could do nothing but tell them to keep back and let them work.

Many ambulances were parked on the road, and many doctors were rushing in. Any that came back out, came out alone.

Sullivan saw one doctor sitting on the edge of an ambulance, his head in his hands.

He considered stopping and making sure the man was okay, but he didn't. He was too angry. This shouldn't have happened. How had no one picked up on this?

Or had someone known, but been too stupid to stop it?

After walking for God-knows how long, he reached a payphone. He stopped, sifted through his pockets for change, and poked a few coins through the slot. It was at times like this a mobile phone would be useful — but he did not want to be tracked, and he despised technology.

He dialled Kelly's number. It rang for a while, but eventually, she answered.

"Hello?"

Sullivan did not speak. He hadn't thought about what he was going to say.

She worked for MI5. She should have stopped this.

"Jay, is that you?" she asked.

He stuttered.

"Jay, please, if that is you, please let me know you're safe."

"I — I'm fine."

"Oh, thank God."

Thank God?

God had fuck all to do with this.

"Did you know?" he asked.

"Pardon?"

He held a breath, his lip curling.

"Did you know?" he repeated.

"Excuse me? Did we know?"

"Yes. Did you know?"

"Are you being serious? Here I am, terrified you are hurt, and you ring me up to accuse me of—"

"You didn't just watch people die."

"You've watched lots of people die, Jay."

Jay went to smash the receiver against the wall, but managed to restrain himself.

"So did you know?"

"No, we did not know."

"*Liar.*"

"Jay, we can talk about this later. In case you hadn't realised, we are busy. So, if you are okay, I will have to go."

"Wait."

He hesitated, regretting being so aggressive.

He let his breathing settle, repressed the bad thoughts, and spoke, his voice low and calm.

"Bring me in," he said.

"What?"

"Bring me in. I want to help."

"You're a wanted man, Jay."

"It doesn't matter."

"I'm afraid it does. In fact, you shouldn't even be talking to me while I'm here."

"It doesn't matter. If you want to do something about this, then you know I'm the right man."

"Jay—"

"I am better than anyone you have at MI5. Bring me in."

"I am not about to admit that I am sleeping with someone on the UK's most wanted list. I'm glad you are okay."

"Fine, I'll go down to the bar on Benton Street. Drink myself stupid. That's the best use for me, isn't it?"

"Goodbye, Jay."

The line went dead.

Sullivan leant against the wall of the phone box and slid to the ground. He remained on the floor, barely moving.

In fact, if it weren't for the steam on the glass caused by his heavy breathing, people walking past might have thought he was dead.

SOUTHEND, UNITED KINGDOM

EIGHT YEARS AGO

CHAPTER EIGHT

At fifteen years old, Zain wasn't what you would call a lad. Nor was he what you would call a petulant teenager, or even a rogue youngster.

He was a faithful son, appreciating all that his parents had done for him. After emigrating from Syria when he was just a baby, they had created a home where Zain would be safe and established themselves as trusted doctors.

His father had always wanted Zain to pursue medicine like he had, but Zain knew he wasn't smart enough. And that was okay. The main thing his father wanted for Zain, or so he said, was happiness.

Only, happiness was something Zain struggled to find. It wasn't a high grade on his exams, it wasn't something he could work for, nor was it something he could buy in a shop.

His friends — who were what you would call lads, petulant teenagers, and rogue youngsters — all told him that he'd find happiness in being one of them. He believed them.

Which meant he also believed them when they told him he should carry a knife. That this place wasn't safe for people like them.

This wasn't for fear of being mugged, or of mistreatment by the police who seemed to bother his friends more than they needed to be bothered.

This was for fear of a group of men who called themselves Paki-Bashers.

Zain hadn't quite believed there was such a thing, at first. I mean, what would be the point? A group of white guys who run around, attacking ethnic minorities with fists and knives. It felt far-fetched.

But this was part of Zain's problem, even though it was something his mother had always found so endearing — he was naive, and desperately so. He saw the best in people. Through his timid nature, he avoided confrontation, and believed that if you just let people be, then they would let you be. Sure, there were probably guys going around and starting shit with those they labelled 'Pakis' — but so long as he didn't interfere with them, they would have no reason to turn their aggression on him. His friends could be a bit confrontational themselves. They were hardly innocent in all this.

Besides, he wasn't even a 'Paki.' He had Syrian origins, not Pakistani — so if these groups of people were, indeed, as they were termed, Paki-Bashers, then they would have no reason to interfere with someone with Syrian roots.

But all of this changed that summer. It was the middle of the holiday, in the sweltering heat of August, and he and his friends were at the local park. Some of them drank, some of them smoked weed, but he just enjoyed the company.

"Bruv, I could get any girl from school," Fahad was saying. "All I have to do is slide up to them and be like... what's up?"

Fahad moved smoothly up to another one of their friends and nudged them with a wink. They all laughed, Zain especially. He didn't necessarily agree with what Fahad was saying, but he found him amusing. A lot of people might think he was a bit of a dick, but he was the one who made friends with

Zain and brought him into the group. He and Fahad were not particularly alike, but they understood each other, and a friendship like they had is rare.

"Did you see that Tiffany girl, she was peng," Fahad continued. He went to continue, but something caught his attention, and he froze.

"Oh, shit," he said.

Zain turned to see what Fahad was staring at.

Across the park was a group of guys, probably a few years older than them, charging around the corner, wearing bomber jackets over tracksuits. Most of them had shaved heads. Most of them were shouting stuff Zain couldn't hear. But all of them, without any exception, had a look on their faces that made Zain panic. It was animalistic, somewhere between a snarl and a growl.

"Let's get out of here," one of his friends said.

"Nah, I ain't leaving," Fahad said, taking a knife from his pocket.

Zain panicked. He'd been worried, but now, seeing this knife, he was terrified.

"Fahad..." he said, cautiously.

"Just go, cuz."

The rest of the crew ran. Zain joined them, then stopped, noticing that Fahad was not running.

"Come on, Fahad!" Zain shouted.

"I ain't going nowhere, fam," Fahad said, standing strong, standing tall.

There were easily eight of them approaching, and some of their shouts were now becoming audible.

"Get off our fucking patch you fucking pakis!"

"No Shariah law in our country!"

"Get the fuck out of here!"

Come on... Zain urged Fahad.

The rest of the group had left the park, but Zain

remained, still yet manic, frantic yet motionless. He was edging toward the exit of the park, but unable to leave without Fahad.

"Fahad!" he shouted. "Let's go!"

Fahad either didn't hear him, or he ignored him.

"Come on!"

Zain heard crying in his voice.

He backed away, seeing the group approach Fahad.

"What the fuck do you want?" Fahad said. "Eh? What the fuck do you want?"

He held his knife out, but it did nothing. He was surrounded.

So many people were in this park, enjoying the lovely day, yet none of them did anything. No one intervened, no one tried to pull the gang away, no one said a thing. The bravest of the voyeurs stood and watched. The rest packed up their picnic and blankets and got the hell out of the park.

Zain noticed one person on their phone, and hoped they were dialling 999.

He wanted to leave the park, but he couldn't. They had surrounded Fahad until Zain could see nothing of his friend, but he could see the punches and the kicks the group were throwing, and he could see that some of them had knives.

Sirens were heard in the distance, and the group seemed to panic. Then the sirens passed. They were clearly not for them, but this was still enough to startle the group. They dispersed, running back in the direction they'd arrived, and had disappeared in seconds.

Fahad was on the floor. He wasn't moving.

All the onlookers did nothing.

Zain ran to Fahad's side, fell to his knees, noticing a large amount of blood coming from Fahad's side. He placed his hands over the blood, trying to stop the flow, like he'd seen done in movies.

But there was another flow of blood coming from further up the body. And another one on the leg.

He tried to cover them also, but he hadn't looked in Fahad's eyes.

If he had, he'd have noticed they weren't moving.

He kept trying to cover the wounds in hope it would save him. He wasn't sure how long he did this for, but eventually a police officer put his arms around Zain's chest and pulled him away.

Later on, the policeman would tell him there was nothing he could have done, and that Fahad had already been dead before Zain got to him.

Zain wouldn't listen to a word this policeman said.

LONDON, UNITED KINGDOM

NOW

CHAPTER NINE

"This is Umar Nasim," Toby said, pointing at a picture taken from CCTV of a nineteen-year-old boy, walking across The Regent's Park toward Camden Market, minutes before the attack. "We believe that he was the suicide bomber."

"Where's he from?" asked Jameson, sitting next to Kelly at the head of the table, with their team spread across either side.

"Birmingham."

"I mean, before that. Where did he emigrate from?"

"Nowhere, he was born in Birmingham. His parents are Bangladeshi, but have lived here for over twenty-five years. He was seen walking into an empty shop an hour before the attack. He was with Huzaifa Nasim, his father, and a known member of Alhami, Naji Qadir."

"Have we got a run-down on Naji Qadir and Huzaifa Nasim?" asked Kelly.

"Not yet."

"What are we waiting for?"

A man to her left said, "I'm on it," then left the room.

"This is Azeer Nadeem." Toby indicated the picture of another man. "He is believed to be the head of Alhami, and the one who organised the attack. He is also the registered owner of the vacant shop Umar left just before the attack."

"So why weren't we monitoring him?" asked a woman toward the front, scribbling away at her notepad. Kelly felt mildly annoyed at her interruption, but it was a relevant question — it was MI5's job to follow suspected terrorists.

"He's in HMP Brenthall," Toby said. "A prison made up of category A and B wings. With him locked up, our intelligence was that Alhami were dormant."

"That's bloody stupid," grunted Jameson. "Someone should still have been monitoring him. Who was doing that?"

Everyone stared at him, but no one spoke.

"Well?"

"I was, sir," said a man a few faces down. "I monitored all of his communications and had no reason to suspect him of planning an attack. It was my recommendation that he wasn't worth pursuing."

"Have you ever been to a prison in this country?"

"No, sir."

"But you are aware of the prison crisis this country is currently facing, yes?"

"Not entirely, sir."

"Jesus Christ."

Seeing Jameson's anger bubbling, Kelly took over.

"Being in prison means nothing," she said. "Most prison inmates have phones on them. We may have monitored his communications, but we won't have monitored any secret phones we do not know about."

"Having looked into this," Toby interjected, "we have discovered that Azeer is sharing a cell with one of his generals, Hasim Nadal."

"How the fuck did that happen?" barked Jameson.

"I — well — the prison officers don't know, do they?"

"It's true," Kelly reassured Jameson. "They won't know, and prisoners ask to share cells with certain people. They'd have no reason to say no."

"They said in their video that there are two more attacks coming," said Toby, "and he is our primary way of knowing where they are. We believe that he only revealed Camden Market as the target yesterday — not even the suicide bomber knew where he was going until then. It seems Azeer does not tell anyone of the target until twenty-four hours before an attack."

"Could we arrest him?" said another subordinate. "Interrogate him?"

"Are you an idiot?" said Jameson.

Again, seeing Jameson's frustration, Kelly took over. "We can't arrest him. He won't talk if we do, and we'll just give away what we know."

"That's the thing I can't get my head around," Toby said, unsurely. "He was one step ahead of us the whole time. How did he do this without us even getting a sniff of it?"

Kelly and Jameson looked at each other. She knew he was thinking the same thing as she was — that Azeer Nadeem had known what intelligence they had.

This could only mean one thing:

Someone in that room was a traitor.

Someone had ensured that no one knew of this attack.

Kelly glanced from one face to the other, all of which were staring back at her. Each person there had been hand-selected by her and Jameson. Each had worked hard for the cause, made huge sacrifices, and helped ensure many terrorist attacks had been prevented.

It would be nearly impossible to know which one of them had done all of that for show.

"Everyone leave," Jameson said decisively. "Now."

The sounds of chairs creaking and sliding across the floor followed. They shuffled out without a word, and Kelly and Jameson were left alone.

"We have a leak," Jameson said.

"It looks like it."

"We can't trust any of them."

Jameson stood, hands in his pockets, and wandered to the window.

Kelly watched him, considering the impact of this. Who knew how much this leak had revealed, or how far they had infiltrated MI5.

Their next move was going to have to remain between her and Jameson, which complicated things. They couldn't run a full operation with just two of them.

"So what do we do?" Kelly said. "We could split up Azeer and his cellmate, or..."

She had a thought.

"Or what?" Jameson said.

"Or we could leave them there."

"So they can organise the next attack?"

"The next attack will come either way, but we know they are discussing the attacks, which gives us an advantage."

"Are you suggested we plant someone in the prison with them?"

"Yes. Put them in the cell next to them, get them to record their conversations and transmit it to us somehow. If they are speaking Arabic, I can translate it."

"It's a good plan, there's just one problem."

"What?"

Jameson folded his arms. Leant against the windowsill.

"If we can't share this plan with anyone, then who do we get to do it?"

Kelly went to answer, but didn't. She considered this.

"We can't trust anyone here," Jameson said, "and we can't

do it, for fear that someone in there may recognise us. We have no one who can blend in."

He was right. They were going to have to use someone outside of MI5. It would have to be someone they could trust.

But who could they trust?

Who could they rely on?

Who would even be capable of doing this?

Kelly, of course, knew exactly who to suggest, but was afraid to do so.

It may not go down well, but this was not a time for thinking about how she came across — it was a time for making decisions for the greater good.

And the best man for a job was currently sitting at a bar on Benton Street, drowning his sorrows in drink.

She paused, took a deep breath, looked down, and said, "I know someone."

CHAPTER TEN

"You are fucking him?" shouted Jameson.

"Would you calm down?"

"Do not tell me to calm down! Never tell me to calm down! Are you a bloody idiot?"

"Henry, please."

"Don't please me! Jay Sullivan is on the UK's most wanted list. He is an incredibly dangerous man. Do you know how many people he's murdered?"

"He was forced into it."

"What?"

"He was brainwashed and manipulated by our government. He's a victim really."

"A victim?" Jameson threw his arms in the air and turned around, landing his hands on his hips. "A fucking victim? A man who has killed at least 200 people is not a victim, he is a serial killer."

"You don't know him."

"Which I am damn grateful for."

"He's the best option."

"I can't believe you even..."

Jameson turned back to the window.

He wasn't sure he had ever been so angry. Kelly was his partner. Had been for ages. He'd overseen her promotion himself, and he had huge respect for her — yet, here she was, fucking a guy the secret service were after.

Did she even know anything about Jay Sullivan?

Jameson had read his file a few years back, when Sullivan absconded and Jameson's curiosity took him. He may have killed many people for the good guys, but he had killed many of the good guys after that. Whilst there was no arguing that the training the Falcons had put him through was brutal, it was no excuse for betraying your country.

Although, as Jameson knew from his experience, such things were rarely as simple as good guys and bad guys. In fact, sometimes the good guys could be real arseholes.

He dabbed his forehead. He was sweating. He took his blazer off, threw it on a chair, and turned back to Kelly, who was staring at him. She was a strong and resilient woman, and had no problem standing her ground, but right now she looked as if she was being told off by a father for kissing the bad boy at school.

His breathing settled. His heart raced a little slower. He felt himself beginning to calm down, and as he did, a sense of rationality entered his thoughts.

He was not pleased with Kelly, but this may be their only option.

Could they trust a man like Sullivan?

And what of his bosses — what would they say when he told them they were using a man they were hunting so desperately?

He wouldn't tell them. They didn't need to know.

Only he and Kelly would know of Sullivan's involvement, and that would be how he'd keep it.

"Never mind," Kelly said. "It was a bad idea, I—"

"No. No, it wasn't." Jameson wiped perspiration from his forehead with his handkerchief. "He's perfect. Bring him in."

CHAPTER ELEVEN

The bar on Benton Street was like any other bar.

As far as Sullivan was concerned, the bar could have been the crème de le crème of amazing bars, or the shittiest, most broken-down pub in all of England, it didn't matter — so long as it served booze.

He sat on a stool and ordered a whiskey. The barmaid placed it in front of him and he drank it down in one, then ordered another.

Kelly had helped him to begin his fight against alcohol addiction. In the little time he had known her, sobriety had felt like a potential future. He hated people trying to help him, but when Kelly helped him, it didn't feel like he was being helped.

But he didn't give a shit about sobriety anymore. Not after that morning.

That's the thing about addiction — never mind how sober you get, an alcoholic is still an alcoholic.

Oh, if his daughter saw him now, how little she would think of him.

He drank the whiskey down and grunted at the barmaid, "Another."

The news played on the television above the bar, showing a reporter standing in front of the police tape Sullivan had crossed a few hours ago. The headlines were the same and they just kept repeating the same information over and over — only the numbers changed.

"Latest figures on the death toll are at 86, with 46 people in intensive care — more than twenty of which are believed to be children."

"Fuck," muttered Sullivan, taking the whiskey without a word of thanks and drinking it like it was water.

"Please, leave us alone," came a Birmingham accent from behind him.

Sullivan turned around to see what was happening. A young family sat at the table, trying to eat their dinner in peace. A father, a mother, and two children young enough to be toddlers. A man with a shaved head stood over them, evidently taking a dislike to this family being Muslims.

"We had nothing to do with what has happened, we just wish to eat our meal without being disturbed," the father said, but timidly.

The man with the shaved head turned to a table behind him, where two other blokes sat. They stood up and joined him.

"Ain't you seen what's happened on the news?" the man persisted.

"Please—"

"You seen it, and you have the nuts to show your face? You dirty fucking scum."

"We have nothing to do with what happened—"

"Nothing to do with it? You fucking kidding me?"

Sullivan slid off his seat and walked toward them. "Hey, why don't you—"

"Is there a Jay Sullivan?" said a voice from behind the bar. Sullivan turned around, annoyed that someone had just shouted his identity across the bar.

The barmaid stood, with a phone held beneath her chin.

"What?" Sullivan said.

"There's a phone call for you."

With a glance back at the skinhead, Sullivan traipsed back to the bar and took the phone.

"Yeah?" he said.

"Jay, is that you?"

It was Kelly.

"Yep."

"I'm going to give you the name of a safe house, can you meet us there in half an hour?"

"You bringing me in?"

"Can you meet us there or not?"

"Fine."

Kelly gave the address and they hung up.

Aware of the family and the racist group of lads still staring at him, he lifted his glass and drained the last drops of whiskey. He placed some cash on the bar then hobbled over to the family and the men standing over them.

"You defending these cunts, eh?" the man said. "Are you telling me—"

Sullivan struck his fist into the man's face, sending him to the floor and knocking him clean out.

The man's friends looked at Sullivan, stuck between shock and fury. Without hesitation, Sullivan strode toward them and smacked the first guy's head against the wall. The man slid down the wall, landing in a slump; not quite unconscious, but not conscious either.

The final man took out a knife and charged at Sullivan. Sullivan took the guy's wrist and twisted it until he dropped the knife into Sullivan's palm. He placed the guy's wrist onto the nearest table and slammed the knife into the middle of his hand.

The man screamed, staring at his hand attached to the wood, blood dribbling down his fingers.

Sullivan took out a wad of cash and handed it to the father.

"Dinner's on me," he said.

He nodded at the father, took some pills to cure the growing pain in his chest, and left.

CHAPTER TWELVE

The safe room was an unused flat on the outskirts of Islington. It was an unremarkable building with unremarkable residents lurking around it. A perfect disguise — no one would ever notice a run-down, empty flat when all the other flats around it were the same.

Sullivan entered and immediately felt uncomfortable. Kelly sat at a table with a welcoming smile, but her partner seemed less eager, sitting back in his chair with his arms folded and a deadened expression on his face.

"This is Henry Jameson," Kelly said. "Why don't you have a seat?"

The low light made the whole situation feel seedier than it needed to be — but Sullivan knew what kind of person Jameson was. Sullivan could read him straight away. This was all about power. That was why Jameson made Kelly introduce him, refused to offer a hand to shake, and filled the room with shadows.

But Sullivan was not an easy man to intimidate. Those who entered a power struggle with Sullivan tended to not come out of it too well.

Sullivan took a seat and looked from Kelly to Jameson.

"Well, what do we know already?" he asked.

"That's top secret," Jameson said stiffly.

"I have a feeling that I'm not here to eat lollipops and candy-canes, so if you plan to use me, I need to know what's up."

Kelly opened an envelope and pushed a picture of a man toward him.

"This is Azeer Nadeem."

"Before we start," Jameson interjected, "I need you to understand — everything we are about to tell you is classified. You are sworn to secrecy, and anything you leak will result in charges being brought—"

"Charges? Your government is trying to kill me, and you are threatening me with charges? Just tell me the damn story."

Kelly explained the situation, including Azeer's prison sentence, the plan to record his conversations, and the intention of Kelly to translate what he says, all so they could find out when and where the next attacks would be.

Throughout the whole explanation, Jameson remained silent.

"Two more attacks in the next thirty days, huh?" Sullivan said. "You think they are bullshitting you?"

"As it stands, we are taking the threat very seriously," Kelly answered.

"Why would he tell us there are going to be more attacks? Why not just do them?"

"He has a mole in the MI5. As far as he's concerned, he's impenetrable, so why not taunt us?"

"And you want to send me into prison to spy on him?"

"Exactly."

"And you're sure you don't want to send me in so I can beat it out of him? I'd enjoy that."

Jameson tutted and rolled his eyes.

"What?" Sullivan said. "MI5 doesn't condone a little torture to get a terrorist to speak? Don't tell me you've never at least dabbled in water boarding."

"MI5 is—"

"An organisation hunting me and you don't even know why."

"We will not be torturing this information out of him, Mr Sullivan," Jameson insisted. "We will be spying, covertly, and that is the limit of your mission. Truth be told, I don't particularly like having you involved. You are our last resort."

"If I'm being drafted in, I'd imagine I'm your only resort."

"Precisely!"

"In which case, you'd better be a little nicer. Otherwise you'll have no options at all."

"When you two are quite done," Kelly interrupted, "we still have more to discuss."

Jameson stood and meandered to the window, where he remained with his back to them.

"What's his deal?" Sullivan said to Kelly, knowing this would wind Jameson up. It was immature, sure, but he couldn't help it.

"We have one major issue we need to cover before we send you in," she said.

"What's that?"

"People may know who you are. Your identity is known to high-ranking government officials, not to mention criminals linked to those you've killed, like terrorists, gangs, traffickers — the list goes on. This means that, for all we know, Azeer Nadeem could know who you are."

"And?"

"And, if we just send you in as a prisoner, they might not buy it."

"So what do you suggest?"

"Henry?" Kelly prompted.

Ah, this was clearly his part of the plan. This should be good.

"We go public with your arrest," Jameson said. "We alert the press, we go on the news, we tell everyone that we have finally captured a government assassin who committed treason and went against his own country. We celebrate that we have caught a serial murderer who absconded and killed his own people. We will make sure it is known that you are caught, so everyone thinks we got you."

"But you have got me, haven't you? This is what you wanted all along."

"This is far from what I want."

"Really? You mean you won't even take just the slightest bit of pleasure showing off to the rest of your MI5 dicks that you caught a man on the UK's most wanted list? Might this even mean another promotion?"

"Feel free to decline involvement, Mr Sullivan. I truly would not mind."

Sullivan turned back to Kelly. "Where did you get this guy?"

"Jay, you need to understand something, and we need to make it really clear," Kelly said.

"And what's that?"

"We are the only people who will know the truth. We will be the only two people able to pull you out in thirty days, assuming this is all over."

"Yes," Jameson said, "so you best not get on our wrong side."

Sullivan lifted an eyebrow, unsure whether or not that was a joke.

He wondered whether taking on this mission would make his daughter proud — then he realised that all Talia would see was a news report about the infamous Jay Sullivan finally being caught.

But he would explain the truth to her someday.

He hoped.

"So when do we begin?" Sullivan said.

"We have arranged to have you in front of a judge in two hours. You will admit guilt and be held in remand while you await sentencing, which will be arranged for after the thirty days are up so as not to interrupt the operation."

"So we still have two hours?"

"Yes."

"Brilliant." He turned to Jameson and grinned. "Fancy a game of Scrabble?"

CHAPTER THIRTEEN

With Jameson on the phone to make the final arrangements, Kelly and Sullivan found themselves with a small amount of time to spare.

She led him into another room and shut the door. He was about to make an ill-timed quip about whether this was the best time for a quickie; then he saw the look on her face and kept his mouth shut.

"Jay..." she said, rushing forward and embracing him.

He took hold of her arms and moved her away from him.

"I'm scared, Jay," she said.

"Scared? Of what?"

"We didn't see this coming. So many people are dead, and we should have known. We should have known..."

She went to embrace him again, but he held her at an arm's distance.

"And now I'm losing you. To prison. I'm scared — what if you don't come back?"

"I'm not going to stay there, am I? It's hardly the Ritz."

"That's not what I mean, Jay. What if it changes you?"

"Changes me?"

Did she really have no idea who she was sleeping with?

If she thought prison was going to change him, she was evidently unaware of all the things he'd done. If anything, prison was where he belonged. It would be where he would flourish, along with all the other murderers and scumbags.

"I just want you to come back as the same person, the man I fell in love with."

Jay frowned and moved away from her.

"Jay?"

"Don't do that."

"What?"

"Don't tell me you're in love with me. I told you to stop that."

"I can't just stop—"

"Don't be so pathetic."

"I am not—"

"Grow up, Kelly. This is not about us being star-crossed lovers, it's about us stopping another attack. I don't give a shit about whether this relationship survives. It's not even a relationship. We are just sleeping together."

Sullivan marched toward the door, took hold of the door handle, and paused.

Maybe that wasn't fair.

But he had told her before — he had specifically said that this was not a relationship, that this was not love. Bad things happened to those who loved him, and if she felt even a little bit of feeling for him, then she was doomed.

He turned back to her, expecting to see her looking upset, but she did not look vulnerable; she looked pissed. Her arms were folded, her stance robust. She was too strong a woman to pander to his weaknesses.

"You're a dick, Jay, you know that?"

"Yes, I do."

"I'm worried about you, and I'm not going to pretend I'm

not," she said. "Azeer Nadeem is a dangerous man. Prison isn't a nice place."

"I'll be fine," he said.

"But—"

"Trust me, I've faced worse."

"Okay," she said. She didn't mean it.

"And you'll be fine without me. You don't need me fucking up your life, anyway. The mission is most important now. If we follow your plan, then we should be able to figure out when the next attack will be and stop it."

"Yeah."

"And I'll be out before you know it."

"Okay."

He hesitated.

"I'm a bastard, Kelly. Please don't start thinking that you love me. You don't really."

"Don't tell me how I'm supposed to feel."

"Just get a grip, yeah? Stop trying to see something that's not there."

She went to reply, then didn't. She opened the door, then paused, looking back to Sullivan.

"You know what, you're right," she said. "You are a bastard. I don't know what I was thinking."

She marched out the door, leaving Sullivan alone.

It wasn't a nice thing to say, but really, pushing her away was the kindest thing he could ever do for her.

She'd understand some day.

STOKE-ON-TRENT, UNITED KINGDOM

SEVEN YEARS AGO

CHAPTER FOURTEEN

It was the first anniversary of Fahad's death, and Zain was angry.

It wasn't so much the death itself that fuelled his anger — that anger had always been there. This was new anger — anger that still had a fresh, unsettling rawness to it. An anger that he had not spent twelve months trying to repress.

This was anger at everyone around him.

His father didn't understand. He'd just moan that all Zain did was charge around the house, puffing his chest out, making dismissive comments to his brothers and sisters. He no longer wanted to play with his younger sister when she got her Lego out — something he so happily did a year ago.

They didn't seem to understand that his friend's murder had changed everything. His mother and father, whilst sympathetic, had begun to run out of the patience they originally had. It was no longer comments of "how are you feeling today" and "what can we do to help?" They had changed to comments such as "you need to start thinking about your own life" and "you are smart, don't waste it."

The resentment he felt made him want to sabotage his

own life just to get back at them; to avoid having a future as a *fuck you* to his parents.

And so it was, at sixteen years old, Zain left school. His GCSE exams came and went, and he made a mild attempt at answering a few questions on a few exam papers, not particularly caring about the results.

The GCSEs were insignificant to him. What was the point in caring about exams in a world like this? GCSEs were a British thing, almost as much as racism or thug culture.

He despised all of those things.

"You must decide what you wish to do now," his father insisted. "The local college is very good, as is the sixth form attached to your school. They will give you the best chance of going to university."

University?

Hah!

Zain had no intention of going to university. What was the point of going to an institution full of white people wondering which quota he was filling by being there — the only difference between the academic and the xenophobic on the street was the level of education behind their racism; the more intelligent weren't less racist, they were just more subtle about it. Did his father really expect him to go to university just to get a job and pay tax to a government who weren't interested in helping someone unless they were rich and white? All you had to do was watch parliament debating on television and play a game of 'spot the ethnic minority' to realise how much British society was set up to keep him quiet, and keep him poor.

He'd bought a knife that came with a holder, one that he could tie around his calf, and he never went anywhere without it.

One of his friends bagged a job in Stoke-On-Trent working for a solicitor's firm. This friend offered to let Zain stay on his sofa, and Zain did not hesitate. He left home, listening to his father and mother's objections, but once he was free of them and on the train, he found silence. He was free. He was liberated.

He and his friend had a good time — at first.

Then, a few weeks after moving, his friend came home from work with his shirt untucked and his blazer over his shoulder, after what must have been a long, hard day, and lost his patience.

"Just fucking look at this place, Zain!" he ranted. "There's fucking beer cans all over the floor, empty plates from a week ago, the place fucking stinks — when are you going to get a job?"

And there it was. The conditional terms of what had appeared to be an unconditional offer. They were no longer two friends sharing a flat. The dynamic changed. It was like he was being lectured by his father again.

He lost another friendship and, once again, had no place in the world. No family to return to, no home to call his own.

He stormed out of the flat, hearing his friend say, "Zain, man, I'm sorry, it's just been a shit day."

He ignored it.

He walked through town with his hood up and hands in his pockets. People crossed the street to avoid him. People glanced, then made sure they didn't make eye contact. Checked their pockets for their keys and phone, clutched their child's hand.

The white people, that is.

Stoke was a multicultural place, and he passed many people who weren't white and didn't seem to give a shit.

He liked that he intimidated the white people. It meant they knew he was not someone to be fucked with.

He approached a group of white lads hanging around on

the street corner. Zain hesitated. Did he need to pass them? Was there any other way around?

No. Screw that.

I ain't going nowhere.

He wasn't a scared little boy anymore. At least, not on the outside. Now, he was a man. He had his knife, and if anyone dared to start shit, he would fuck them up. He'd gut them all if he had to, then he'd grin at the judge as they handed down a sentence harsher than they would give any of those fuckers, and he would laugh in their face. No one can tell him what to do.

No one.

He took a deep breath, flexed his fingers, paying attention to the feel of his knife strapped to his leg.

He sped up. Glared at them. Eyeballing each of them.

One of them turned to look at him.

This was it.

Got to get ready.

Here we go.

Then the man turned away. Looked back at his friends, and continued laughing. No one else looked at him. They were oblivious. They didn't give a shit.

Zain walked past them, keeping his head turned so he could see if they charged at him over his shoulder.

But they didn't.

He carried on walking, and realised how tense his body had become. He breathed out and felt his whole body relax.

His arms were shaking.

What was happening to him?

He turned the corner. A mosque came into view.

He'd go there. He always found comfort in his mosque in Southend. There would always be an imam willing to listen.

Not that he had anything he particularly wanted to say, he

just wanted someone willing to listen to whatever came out once he began ranting.

So he entered.

Walked through the doorway, not knowing that this decision was going to change his entire life.

Not knowing that he was about to meet a powerful man by the name of Azeer Nadeem.

LONDON, UNITED KINGDOM

NOW

CHAPTER FIFTEEN

KELLY AND JAMESON STOOD ALONE IN THEIR OFFICE, ignoring the hustle and bustle occurring outside. People were still rushing back and forth, tapping frantically at their keyboards, carrying out their jobs.

None of them had any idea that their best hope lay in an alcoholic ex-assassin.

They watched the news report together and, as they did, Kelly tried to ignore the sick feeling that rose through her stomach.

"The government has announced the capture of one of the most notorious and elusive men on their most-wanted list, a man by the name of Jay Sullivan," said the news reporter.

They cut to a video of Sullivan, his hands in handcuffs, being led out of a van and into a courthouse.

"This was the scene earlier as he entered London Crown Court, where he pleaded guilty to treason and six counts of murder of British officials. The judge declared that he would be held at HMP Brenthall while he awaits sentencing."

They showed a mugshot of Sullivan — one Kelly had

taken and leaked to the press before Sullivan was driven to court.

"The government have as yet been unwilling to comment on the accusation that they used Jay Sullivan as a hitman, both in the UK and abroad, up until seven years ago. Our sources, however, suggest that he was used in covert operations until he turned against his own government, and murdered some of his superiors."

They showed the van driving into HMP Brenthall and the doors shutting behind it.

"These are images from moments ago when Jay Sullivan arrived at HMP Brenthall. Prison officials have said that he will be denied a cell mate and given close watch due to the risks they believe he poses to others."

The television returned to the news reporter.

"It is unclear how the government used to use a man like this — but it is clear the dangers he poses to the British public. For now, at least, the public can feel safe knowing that one of the country's most dangerous men is behind bars, and is unlikely to ever be let out."

The news report finished. Kelly turned off the television and wandered to the window, looking at the busy street below. She put her hands in her pockets, and avoided looking at Jameson.

Jameson wasn't looking at her either. He was standing, his arms folded, in deep contemplation.

Kelly considered Sullivan. The news report had brought a sense of reality to their relationship — if that's what it was, what with Sullivan being so desperate to insist that they were not in a relationship, and nor would they ever be — and she began to wonder... how well did she actually know Jay Sullivan?

He said he'd absconded for the right reasons, and they hadn't discussed the matter further. She knew what the

Falcons were like, and she had little respect for their operations. But had her feelings toward him clouded her judgement?

Did she really trust him enough to carry out this mission?

Was it right that they were putting all of their hope into the competency of a man who must surely hold a deep grudge against his own government?

She covered her face. Huffed. Bit her lip.

She wished she'd thought this through.

"What is it?" Jameson said, seeing the look on her face.

"I — it's just..." She hesitated. "I just hope we know what we're doing."

Jameson nodded.

"Me too, Kelly. Me too."

CHAPTER SIXTEEN

THE VAN WAS HOT AND SULLIVAN WAS SWEATING THROUGH his shirt. He told himself it was okay, he could just get his suit dry-cleaned — then remembered that he couldn't. In fact, he wouldn't see this suit again for a while.

Even if he were allowed to wear his own clothes, a luxury not usually given to new prison entrants, he would have to wear the kind of clothes inmates would wear. Something like ... a tracksuit.

His face screwed up in disgust. What a horrid thought.

There were no windows in the van, so he couldn't be sure where he was — but they were starting to slow down. Sullivan assumed that they were now entering the prison.

The van continued at a slow pace, then came to a stop. A moment passed and the backdoors opened. Three prison officers waited for him. A woman, short and overweight, in uniform — white shirt, black trousers, and a belt with keys and radio — and two men who seemed to trail behind her. Sullivan had expected a larger entourage to greet him, but thousands of prison officers' jobs had been cut in the last few years and this was what they'd been reduced to. He couldn't help but feel bad for them — if he wished to start something, they stood no chance. He wondered just how safe this meant life was going to be inside.

"Come on," the woman barked, and led him off the van. He followed her through a corridor to a desk, where they paused, the two male officers remaining behind him.

"Your name is Jay Sullivan, correct?" she asked, her voice consistently monotone, like she was reciting words she'd learnt so long ago she'd forgotten their meaning.

He nodded.

"You have been found guilty of murder and are to wait here for sentencing, which is scheduled for the twenty-eighth of next month. Do you understand this charge?"

He nodded.

"Do you smoke?"

He shook his head.

"Do you have an addiction to drugs, including spice, cannabis, or any other?"

He shook his head.

"Do you have any mental health issues?"

He shook his head.

"Have you or do you feel like you are going to self-harm, commit suicide, or harm others?"

He shook his head.

"Sign here."

She placed three pieces of paper in front of him. He signed them without reading them.

He placed the pen down and she said, "Follow me," then led him to a holding cell. She held the door open and he walked in, then listened to the sound of the heavy door being shut and locked behind him.

He imagined he'd have to get used to that sound.

He stood in the cell for a few minutes, reminding himself why he was doing this.

I could murder a whiskey, he thought.

Half an hour later, the cell door was open, and a prison officer stood there, a man this time.

"Come with me," he said. He was tall, bald, and looked too old for this.

Sullivan followed him through to a small, private room, where another male officer awaited them, holding a box.

"Put any possessions or items you have in this box," the man told him.

"I don't have any," Sullivan replied.

"The suit," the man prompted.

Ah, the suit.

He wished he could say a longer goodbye to it. He told himself it was only going to be thirty days; just one month, then he could have it back.

He removed his tie. Took off his blazer. Undid his shoelaces and handed them over. Removed the shirt. The trousers.

The man placed them carelessly in the box, not caring about how much he was creasing it.

"Remove your underwear," the man instructed.

Sullivan glared at him.

"Trust me, I don't want to see it any more than you want to show it," the man said.

"Fuck's sake," Sullivan muttered under his breath, and dropped his underwear to his ankles.

"Bend over."

This was ridiculous. Sullivan did not appreciate someone telling him what to do — in fact, it infuriated him — and it was only made worse by the humiliation of having a man shine a light into his arsehole.

Forever one for the inopportune moments for humour, Sullivan looked over his shoulder at the man inspecting his crevasse and asked, "Any chance you're going to buy me a beer after this?"

"You can't have beer in prison," the man replied, his voice monotone and his face blank.

"Fuck," Sullivan said. He feared hearing such a thing.

"Sit on the boss chair," the prison officer instructed him.

Sullivan assumed he meant the only chair in the room. It was a solid chair made up of squares and rectangles, and was plugged into the wall.

He sat on it. After a moment, the check was done, and he was allowed to stand.

"Put these on."

They handed him prison uniform, and he decided this was the most humiliating part of all. He snatched them off the prison officer and reluctantly put them on. They were baggy and stank of damp.

He was taken into another room, where he was asked the same questions again, and had to continually insist that he was not an addict, nor was he about to harm himself.

He was given a card. On it was his picture, his prison number, his name, and date of birth.

Finally, he was led through another corridor, and told to wait outside an office.

After a few minutes, the door opened, and his name was called.

He walked inside.

CHAPTER SEVENTEEN

"Is it normal for you to meet all new inmates?" Sullivan asked.

The prison governor, Jason Patricks, smiled back at him. He was a short man with poorly combed hair and an ill-fitted suit, coming across as patronising as he did arrogant, yet still managed to carry an air of authority with him.

"Not usually," he said. "But there are some inmates I wish to meet. The high-profile ones. The ones I believe are most likely to cause us issues."

"And that's me, is it?"

"Well, you tell me."

Sullivan hated this kind of conversation. It was like they were measuring dicks. What's more, Sullivan did not like people trying to get one up on him, or condescending to him, or treating him like an idiot.

But he was going to have to take it. He needed to show that he wasn't going to be any trouble, even if his instinct was to leap over the table and break the guy's arm.

"You are guilty of multiple counts of murder. You are yet to be sentenced, but you must know you're in here for life —

meaning you would lose nothing by trying to escape. This makes you a dangerous man. Are you a dangerous man, Mr Sullivan?"

Sullivan grinned. "You have no idea."

"I have also noticed that we have been instructed to place you in a particular cell. Cell 35 on E wing. Considering your charges, I would like to put you on a category A part of the prison, and E wing is category B. This seems a little strange."

Sullivan let a moment of silence linger before asking, "Is there meant to be a question in there?"

"Just a warning. Should you give me any reason to move you to a more appropriate location, then I will be quite within my rights. Do you understand?"

Oh, did Sullivan's blood boil.

'Do you understand?'

His rage sang a symphony in his mind, but he had to avoid lashing out. He had been placed in that cell to monitor the man in the cell next to it. If he was moved, even temporarily, he could miss out on vital intel.

"Fine," he grunted.

"Excuse me?"

"I said fine."

"Wonderful. Now I know that we have an understanding, I will have my officer take you to your cell on E wing. All the best, Mr Sullivan."

Sullivan wanted to break the guy's nose.

"Sure."

Sullivan stood to leave, then paused, noticing something on the wall. It was a picture of Patricks shaking the hand of a familiar man. The man was younger, slightly less grumpy, and a little thinner, but it was unmistakably Henry Jameson. They appeared to know each other.

The prison officer collected him and gave him a welcome box for him to carry. Inside it was a blanket for his bed, a chocolate bar, and some kind of pamphlet about prison life and rules. He was led through a few corridors until they emerged into a courtyard full of prisoners, some moseying around, some sitting and talking, some exercising.

A few prison officers rushed past them, and Sullivan noticed a fight had broken out.

"I'll be right back," the officer told Sullivan; it seemed he would have to wait to be shown to his cell.

As he waited, he took in the horrid location that was now his home, gazing at the faces of the people who he never wanted to mix with, never mind live with.

As he did, he felt a pair of eyes on him.

He paused. Turned around.

There he was.

Sat on a bench with his cronies gathered around him. Leader of his gang. Murderer of many.

Azeer Nadeem.

He was short, but had muscle. He looked like he could handle himself but, by the look of his disciples around him, he looked like he'd never need to.

Sullivan held his glare.

It intensified, neither wanting to break it.

"I'll be seeing you," Sullivan said, knowing only he could hear it.

"Come on," said the prison officer, appearing at Sullivan's side, the scrap evidently dealt with.

He held the stare a moment longer, then broke it, following the officer to the cell on E wing that would be his home for the next thirty days.

Thirty long, arduous days.

He couldn't imagine what it would be like to have to stay there permanently.

STOKE-ON-TRENT, UNITED KINGDOM

SIX YEARS AGO

CHAPTER EIGHTEEN

Zain sat at the back of the room, listening to Azeer speak, finding his pen absentmindedly doodling. Before long, the cover of his pamphlet was covered in drawings of guns, bombs, tanks and warplanes.

Azeer didn't talk much in the mosque. No one ever shunned him or said anything disparaging, yet he always seemed to be isolated from everyone else; there was an air of disapproval toward him.

But when Azeer taught his religious study group on a Saturday afternoon, he finally had the audience he deserved — a group of eager eight to twelve-year olds, all dropped off by equally eager parents, wishing for them to learn about what Azeer had to say.

So when Azeer had asked Zain to help out in his classes, Zain had been more than enthusiastic.

There was something enchanting about Azeer, something that a lot of people didn't see — but those that did see it were all the better for it. When he spoke, his audience was captivated. When he delivered his messages, he did so with such clarity and charisma that you couldn't help but listen.

Zain had never had this kind of confidence. He had always retreated to the back of the classroom, or watched his friends as they showed off to girls. He had never been able to capture an audience.

But Azeer… everything he said was so well delivered, and he did it with such allure. Zain couldn't help but envy it.

"So we have enemies," Azeer was saying. "Some say we don't, but those people are non-believers. And what does the Quran say about those that don't believe?"

One of the children shot his hand into the air.

"Yes?" said Azeer.

"Those who believe fight in the cause of Allah, and those who disbelieve fight in the cause of Taghut. So fight against the allies of Satan."

"Brilliant," Azeer said, smiling with such enthusiasm that the child couldn't help but beam with pride. "And if those who disbelieve fight for Satan, then those are the enemy, are they not?"

An eager murmur of "yes" answered him.

"And if these people do not believe in the glory of Allah, how can they end up going any way but Satan's way?"

He put a hand on his chin like he was thinking.

Zain loved this part — it was a brilliant performance, and the children always bought into it.

"And who can tell me what an infidel is?"

A child put his hand up. "Someone who doesn't believe in Allah."

"And what does the Quran have to say about that?"

Another child put her hand up. "And when the sacred months have passed, then kill the polytheists wherever you find them and capture them and sit in wait at every place of ambush."

"Couldn't have quoted better myself." Azeer rewarded the girl with a few sweets. "But, remember, we are still forgiving

— if they should repent, establish prayer and give zakah, let them go their way. Indeed, Allah is forgiving and merciful. And he is, isn't he?"

They all nodded.

"If Allah will forgive them, then he is truly glorious, isn't he?"

They all nodded again.

"And what does the Quran say we should do to those who do not believe in Allah?"

The same child who had just answered put her hand up again.

"Oh, you are doing well today. Go on."

"Fight those who believe not in Allah or the Last Day, nor acknowledge the religion of truth."

"Exactly! And if they can't acknowledge the religion of truth…" He showed an expression of disgust. "Then what do we do?"

"We fight," said every child in unison.

Even Zain found himself saying the answer with them.

"We will always fight against those who try to oppress Islam. Who can give me an example of this?"

"Israel!" shouted one child.

"Good! Where the Palestinians were oppressed by Israel. Another?"

"Myanmar!" shouted another child.

"Perfect — where Rohingya Muslims are oppressed! Another?"

"Serbia!"

"Exactly — where Bosnian Muslims are killed."

Zain became excited. His part was almost here.

"And who are our biggest enemies? Who has hurt us most?"

Silence. Each child looked like they wished they could answer, but just couldn't.

"Zain," said Azeer. "Tell me some facts."

He put his pamphlet down and sat forward. All the children turned to look at him, and he made sure he did not let Azeer down.

"When Al Quaeda crashed into the Twin Towers in 2001, 2,977 people died."

"That's a lot, isn't it? But it's not everything. Zain, how many innocent people did America and the UK kill in Iraq?"

"We don't know for sure."

"Why not?"

"Because they won't tell us the truth."

"Because they won't tell us the truth!" Azeer folded his arms and shook his head. "But if we choose to believe them, how many innocent civilians do they admit to killing?"

"In April 2003, it was 7,419."

"Isn't that more than twice the 2,977 you just said died on September 11th?"

"It is."

"And those are just the ones they admit to?"

"Yes, Azeer."

"And in the Afghanistan war? How many killed there?"

"More than 26,000 civilians, almost nine times as many as on September 11th."

Azeer said nothing. He looked to the children, shaking his head in disbelief, allowing those numbers to linger.

He looked at each curious set of eyes, at each avid listener awaiting his conclusion.

"And the worst part of this," said Azeer, taking another pause for emphasis, "is that they dare to call *us* the terrorists."

The children joined in Azeer's disbelief, shaking their heads.

Zain thought back to Fahad. Had that group of men who had killed his friend been terrorists? Azeer believed so.

And what about those other Muslims at the mosque who shunned Azeer for his beliefs?

They evidently had not heard the figures Zain had just quoted.

They evidently did not see the sense in what Azeer was saying.

And they evidently did not have a clue what they were talking about.

HMP BRENTHALL, UNITED KINGDOM

NOW

CHAPTER NINETEEN

Oh, what Sullivan would do to return to one of those luxurious hotels he used to stay in. Occasionally, he'd stay in a run-down motel after a particularly high profile killing to be discreet — but, most of the time, he would stay in the classiest of establishments. He didn't have a home for most of his career, he just stayed in fancy hotel after fancy hotel, with pristine sheets, glorious room service, and the most expensive furniture a business could afford.

This prison cell made the run-down motels look like one of the luxurious hotel rooms.

There was a sink in the corner, next to a toilet that had nothing but a small curtain to provide its user with some dignity. The bed had the thinnest mattress Sullivan had ever laid on, and as a new entrant to the prison, he was not yet provided with a duvet — he was provided with a blanket. There was a small table, but it was so close to the bed that Sullivan would have to sidestep to get past it. The cell did have a television, one that still had the big back that televisions had in the nineties, but Sullivan didn't turn it on. He needed to listen for sounds in the cell next to his.

He waited for night to descend, sure that Azeer wouldn't plan for Alhami's next attack until people were asleep. He lay on the bed, ignoring the way the springs of the mattress dug into his back, and wondered how likely it was he'd have ended up in one of these places permanently had the Falcons not recruited him.

That was one positive about the Falcons — they did stop him from turning to a life of crime.

Then again, did they? Did a life of assassinating people not count as a life of crime?

It's strange. All you have to do is put a weapon in a man's hand and call him a soldier, then suddenly their killing is an act of heroism, not murder.

That's what Alexander had called him, at first. A soldier.

It had felt good.

He was a troubled young man who was unlikely to have been allowed into the army. Even so, his father had always emphasised the importance of Armistice Sunday and honouring fallen soldiers. Despite his father being an abusive bastard, he was also a highly regarded police officer. He believed in the troops, and he ensured Sullivan believed in them too.

In fact, the only thing that would have made his father proud was if Sullivan became a soldier. Maybe his father would have taken a break between the beatings to congratulate him.

Then again, there was probably nothing he could have done to change his father's sadistic ways — as he learnt when his father killed Sullivan's mother before turning the gun on himself.

"What does a soldier do?" Alexander had said to Sullivan's eighteen-year-old self, in a conversation following a day of combat training.

"Uh, I don't know," was Sullivan's instinctive, adolescent

response. He squinted at the sun, sweating considerably following his day's workout.

"Humour me."

"Well they, er, they kill things."

"So does a serial killer, Jay. Be more specific."

"They kill enemies."

"Whose enemies?"

"Our country's enemies."

"Precisely! And what would happen if they didn't kill them?"

"Then innocent people would die."

"And does a soldier need an explanation as to why they are killing their enemy?"

"No. A soldier is taught to follow orders."

"Why?"

"So that innocent people would live."

"And are you a soldier?"

"Yes."

"Are you our soldier?"

"Yes."

"You are a smart man, Jay. A truly smart man."

"But how do we know who the enemy is? Is it always so obvious?"

Alexander took a moment to consider this.

"Sit with me," he said, indicating a bench.

He sat, and Sullivan followed.

"The short answer is that you know who the enemy is because we tell you who the enemy is," Alexander said. "Because we have people who spend day after day investigating and analysing intelligence, and it is not always so simple to explain to you what has taken months, or even years, to deduce. It is not up to the soldier to understand how the intelligence has been used, or how we have made the inferences we've made."

Alexander loosened his top button and undid his collar.

"But, for now, let's entertain the long answer, shall we?"

Sullivan nodded.

"Where were you on September 11th, 2001?"

"I don't know. At school, probably."

"See, I can remember exactly where I was and what I was doing. I was not at work that morning, as my daughter had a temperature. I'd just brought her some soup when I put on the news and saw it. 2,977 people died that day, Jay. What about on 7th July 2005?"

Sullivan shrugged. "No idea."

"I could tell you everything about the attack on that day. Mohammad Sidique Khan, Shehzed Tanweer, Hasib Hussain and Germaine Lindsey drove in a rental car from Bedfordshire to London. They set off four bombs — three on the underground, one on a bus. And do you know how old the youngest of them was?"

"No."

"Eighteen. Just like you are now. Hasib Hussain was eighteen, and he killed himself to attack us. Just think about that for a second."

Alexander paused to let that settle.

"Does that not fill you with anger? Does that not fill you with rage?"

"I guess so."

"And if we spent days going through all the intelligence we had before sending you to assassinate Hasib Hussain, would that make you feel any better about doing it?"

"No."

"Would that change anything?"

"No."

"No, it would not. It is not your job to sift through the intelligence. That's ours. It's your job to kill men like this, save lives, and stop asking so many damn questions. Always remember — we do it for the greater good."

Sullivan nodded. He understood.

Bad men had to die.

It was his job to ensure that.

For the greater good, of course.

Always for the greater good.

"Go," Alexander said. "Get to the showers before they are all taken."

Sullivan stood.

"Oh, and Jay?"

"Yeah?"

"You're doing great."

He nodded and left.

Lying in the prison cell, Sullivan could still hear Alexander's words. That phrase, *the greater good.*

What did those words even mean?

What was so great about *good* anyway?

Many atrocious, evil acts of genocide have been committed in the name of good.

A shuffle came from the cell next to his.

He sat up, listening intently.

Some talking began. It was Arabic. Even though it was one of the few languages Sullivan didn't speak, he recognised it. He'd spent enough time in the Middle East to be able to pick out certain words, such as hadi, which meant quiet, and albab, which meant door.

He returned to the box he had been given when entering the prison and withdrew a small box of cereal. Some inmates who had been given responsibility for putting the welcome packs together, and Kelly had told Sullivan that she'd paid one of them to ensure this particular box of cereal ended up in his welcome pack.

Sure enough, he opened the cereal box and found exactly

what he needed. A Dictaphone, and a piece of paper with COLO5684 written on it.

"Your cell is close enough to the prison wall that the Dictaphone will connect via Bluetooth to a Dictaphone hidden in a bin outside it," Kelly had told him. "Make sure the recordings are transferred by 10:00 a.m., as our contact will collect the files shortly after."

He found the device called COLO5684, and paired the Dictaphones.

He was not particularly good with technology, but it was easy enough.

He stood on the chair, pressed it against the wall to get the clearest sound, and hit record.

CHAPTER TWENTY

JUST AS THEY DID EVERY NIGHT, AZEER AND HASIM WAITED for the cells to be locked and silence to descend. Shouting routinely continued into the night, with the psychotics and the crazies objecting to the way the walls closed in on them, or declaring which officer was a prick, or repeating whichever racial slur had become the new fad.

Eventually, the dead of night would approach and the shouting would cease. After at least thirty minutes of silence, they would confer, their voices hushed, discussing what needed to be discussed in Arabic for extra security.

Hasim said, quietly, "Saar alarm 'ala nahw jayyed." *It went well*.

"Kam 'adad alwafayat?" *How many deaths?*

"'Akthar min thamanin." *More than eighty*.

Azeer sat on his bed and leant back, allowing himself a bit of pride. The demonstration at Camden Market had been carried out beautifully. The death toll was rising, and Allah's work was being done.

Azeer had also been assured that the video had been released to the appropriate government agencies — a video that was filmed over a year ago, when the preparation for this glorious month had begun.

Now the British government would know this was only the beginning. There were still two more demonstrations left, and nothing could stop them now. No one appeared to suspect Azeer or Hasim; no police, no MI5, nothing. No one had come to arrest them, nor had anyone even brought them in for questioning.

Azeer wasn't getting carried away, however, and was aware that the British authorities could just be taking a few days to plan their arrests and subsequent interrogations. Even so, it didn't particularly matter; their martyrs were highly trained and well prepared. Even if someone did come along and try and torture the times and locations out of him, they would get nothing, and his men would complete their mission regardless.

The best part? The country was still reeling from the first demonstration, and the second would come along almost as soon as the first.

They would have no idea what to do.

Hasim asked, "Hal nahnu musta'edoun?" *Are we ready?*

Azeer wondered whether they should stretch out the glory of what had happened in Camden Market for a little longer. It was a great moment, and he wanted to revel in it.

But he could revel in even more devastation by giving the go ahead for the next demonstration.

Azeer replied, "Nem." *Yes.*

It was now up to Hasam to send the message.

Hasam lifted the sink and collected the iPhone that was hidden beneath. He turned it on and waited for the home screen to appear.

"Ma howa azzaman walmakan?" he asked. *What is the time and place?*

Azeer gave the location and the day to Hasim. Hasim sent the text.

He returned the phone to its hiding place beneath the sink and nodded at Azeer.

Azeer leant back on his bed and gazed above. He imagined he was looking at the stars, even though he was staring at a stained ceiling that was once a sickly cream colour, and was now a dirty mess.

He imagined the glory he would have when the next part of the mission went well. He pictured success, and he imagined the British intelligence services running around helplessly with no idea when or where the next demonstration was.

That was why he sent the video. To taunt them. To make them feel helpless. So they would realise how much power Alhami had, and would know how much they had underestimated Azeer Nadeem. They would know they could not repress the Islamic state any longer.

Azeer would turn on the television in a few days and marvel at the destruction.

And then they would prepare for the biggest attack.

The country would be on edge, already devastated by two demonstrations, with no idea how bad it could get.

CHAPTER TWENTY-ONE

THE PRISONERS WERE ALLOWED OUT OF THEIR CELLS FOR AN hour each day. They could wander, play pool, exercise in the courtyard, or any other activity they could think of to alleviate the monotony.

Sullivan kept himself to himself and, after three or four days, fell into a routine.

He would begin the day by waking up in a pool of sweat with a pounding headache. His stomach would feel acidic and he'd struggle to eat. His hands would shake and he would close his eyes, waiting for it to pass. He knew this would happen. You weren't allowed alcohol in the prison and he was quickly learning what his body did without it.

The symptoms would usually quell slightly after he'd had coffee and some water — either that, or he just grew accustomed to it.

Then he would try exercising. A few push-ups, a few press-ups, some running on the spot. Anything to kill the time.

Lunchtime would arrive. He'd be starving, but the food only made his stomach worse. That wasn't necessarily because of the nausea caused by lack of booze, but because he wasn't used to such inedible sludge.

Then they would be allowed out of their cell. They were supposed to get an hour, but it would depend on the mood of whichever screw was on shift — screw being a term used by inmates when referring to a prison officer. He disliked using more words than he had to, so he welcomed the chance to just use a single syllable to describe these people.

While he was out of the cell, he would wander around, watching the inmates, subtly keeping his attention on Azeer and his comrades. After a short walk, he would sit on the same bench — a bench which soon became his bench. No one else would go near it, as if it was understood that it was his.

They'd have all seen the news. They'd know who he was, and what he had done. Only a fool would want to fuck with him.

Once the hour in the courtyard was up, he would return to his cell, where the rest of the afternoon and evening would be spent watching the news. He often thought about calling Kelly — not for a discussion about work, but for a chat. To see how she was doing. To see whether or not his being a prick had done its job of pushing her away.

But he couldn't call her. If someone saw records of him phoning an MI5 agent it could rouse suspicion.

Eventually, the night would come. He would retrieve the Dictaphone from its hiding place and, despite the voices being so faint he could barely hear them, he would record.

Then he would sleep, get up, and the day would repeat.

But, on this particular day — the fourth day Sullivan had counted — he walked into the courtyard to find his normally empty bench occupied.

Azeer sat on it, with the rest of his group sat around him, puffing out their chests, strutting around, acting tough.

Sullivan knew why they were there.

It was his bench, and they knew it. They were hanging around it to ensure that the new inmate knew exactly where he stood. They needed to show Sullivan that, despite being a known murderer, he was not in charge.

At this point, Sullivan had a choice to make. Did he let them keep the bench? Or, did he refuse to allow them to have authority over him?

He knew he should just leave it. He knew he shouldn't start anything. He knew that, should he get into a fight, he could be moved cells.

Yet, being the person he was, and feeling the anger he felt when looking at this piece of shit, his ego struggled to let it go.

Just go, just leave it, just—

Azeer caught his eye. Noticed Sullivan staring. Azeer glared back, and the rest of his crew turned too.

Rage rose through Sullivan. This was the man who planned to kill more people in a few seconds than Sullivan had in a lifetime.

And he'd killed Sajid.

One of his own.

A sweet kid.

Would he see Sajid as a necessary sacrifice? Or would he decide Sajid deserved it for not having the same extreme ideologies as him?

Or would he even give a fuck at all?

"You got a problem?" asked the man next to Azeer. Sullivan recognised the voice as Hasim's, the man who shared a cell with Azeer.

Sullivan did not reply. He just continued his glare with Azeer.

Azeer grinned.

"He asked you a question," he said.

Sullivan shook his head. "You guys are a joke."

"What did you say?"

"I said you guys are a joke."

Azeer stood, as did the rest of his group, squaring up to him, looking all tough and hard — to everyone else, that was, but Sullivan.

He could feel eyes turning. People aiming uncomfortable glances in their direction.

"You're on my bench," Sullivan said.

"This is your bench?" Azeer replied.

"Yes. Yours is over there."

He pointed to the bench they normally sat on.

"Yeah, that's not how I see it. I see this bench, that bench, that bench, that bench — and all of them belong to me, and I can sit on whichever one I like."

"Is that so?" Sullivan said.

"Yes, it is. And what you got to say about it?"

Sullivan smiled back. He looked at Hasim, then scanned the eyes of the rest of Azeer's group of sheep, before turning back to their leader.

He reminded himself to lay low. To avoid trouble. He did not want to get moved cells. Breaking Azeer's skull would probably not be a good idea.

"Look at you," said Azeer, moving to within inches of Sullivan's face. "Big white boy trying to get us Muslims to move. Don't like us Asians."

"I couldn't give a shit whether you're brown, white, black or orange — I just want my bench."

"Oh yeah? Then take it."

Azeer waited for Sullivan to make a move.

Sullivan stared back at Azeer, paying particular attention to what Azeer was doing with his hands. Sullivan had no doubt that, should he swing his fist, Azeer would have something sharp ready to retaliate, probably made out of a toothbrush or a pair of scissors.

A whistle went, interrupting their exchange.

"Inside!" shouted a screw.

Azeer laughed in Sullivan's face.

"Fucking gweilo," he muttered, and pushed Sullivan out of the way.

Sullivan was forced to step aside, and it took every piece of self-control in his body not to grab the hand that pushed him and snap it off.

Azeer chuckled, Hasim chuckled, as did the rest as they barged into him and walked on.

Sullivan watched them go. He kept his eyes on them until they disappeared into their cells, and he disappeared into his.

Oh, how much he would love to show them who the bigger man was.

He reminded himself of the greater good. Of the lives they were trying to save.

Although, at that moment, he didn't care — all that mattered was destroying this man, one way or another.

CHAPTER TWENTY-TWO

Kelly downloaded the files onto the computer, just as she did every day, and loaded them into her audio software.

Sometimes she wondered if there would be a message before the recordings began, or after they finished, where Sullivan would say that he was okay, or that he hoped she was okay, or that he missed her, or...

But of course there wasn't.

He would never be that kind of boyfriend. As he kept on insisting, he wasn't even her boyfriend. He was just a man she was fucking.

Maybe he was right.

Or maybe his past had really damaged him and he needed her support.

Or maybe he'd change his mind someday.

Or maybe...

I don't know.

"Stop it," she told herself, then huffed.

The same monotonous routine began. The recordings were quiet, so she had to alter it. She highlighted the audio tracks, selected *noise reducer,* then decreased the noise to its lowest decibel. She would select *amplify* and increase the volume to the maximum. Finally, she would export that into another file, re-import it, and use *amplify* to increase the volume again.

Then she would have what she was after — a perfectly audible file.

Well, not perfectly audible. She still had to strain a little.

She would play a sentence, write it down on her pad, then type up the translation. Play a sentence, write it down, type it up. Play, write, type; play, write, type — and so forth.

Every day she heard the same back and forth between Azeer Nadeem and Hasmin Nadal, and the same diatribe about how the British would pay for repressing the Islamic state — something Kelly thought was unlikely to actually be a priority on the government's list of tasks.

Sometimes she thought about her next-door neighbours. They were Muslim. She often had them around for dinner. There was never any tension between them, and never even any mention of religion. She ensured what she cooked was halal, but that was the only thought she ever gave to their beliefs.

It reassured her that Azeer Nadeem was the exception, not the rule.

She had considered inviting her neighbours around to meet Sullivan, in fact. But then she realised what a stupid idea that was. Meeting her friends for dinner was a 'boyfriend' thing — not something Sullivan would ever agree to.

Was she foolish to keep hoping he would change his mind? She considered herself to be a strong, independent woman, and felt pathetic for constantly hoping she could break down his barriers and convince him that they were in love.

Shut up, Kelly.

She needed to stop thinking about this. She needed to focus.

It was hard to do so, admittedly, as everything she listened to was repetitive and gave them nothing.

It was day after day of the same thing, never getting anywhere. This was a task she'd usually dictate to someone else but, being unable to trust their team, she had to do it. It was the same job she'd done when she'd left the marines and started out at MI5 as an Arabic to English translator. She'd come a long way since then, yet, sitting here doing it again, she felt like she hadn't come a long way at all.

She made herself a coffee then continued, reminding herself that this was the only way. This task could provide the intelligence they needed to prevent more deaths.

But she found nothing, after nothing, after nothing — until the moment came when she finally found something.

Until she finally heard what she had been waiting to hear.

A location.

She opened a new notepad and wrote it down.

She kept listening. The time had to be next. It had to be.

Just more talk. More waffling. More discussions.

She sped up, then told herself to slow down.

She had to be astute. Careful. Had to listen to everything.

Then they said it. The day.

"Shit, we have it!"

She wrote it on the notepad, and leapt up.

She knew when and where the attack would be.

CHAPTER TWENTY-THREE

Kelly bounced around the room, almost unable to decide what to do first, leaping from one foot to the other

They could stop it. They could actually stop this attack. Unlike the fuck up of a week ago, they could prevent it from happening.

She picked up her phone. Called Jameson.

"Get in here right now," she said.

"Do we know—"

"We know, just hurry."

She hung up and stared at the pad. She felt proud. Eager. Keen.

Then she gave herself a reality check — she had only found the time and location. They hadn't stopped it yet. There was still work to do.

Jameson entered minutes later, shutting the door behind him.

"I had to leave my meeting early for this, please tell me you're not fucking with me."

"I am not fucking with you."

She turned the pad toward him, and he read aloud.

"Brighton Pier."

"Yep."

"The day of the night the clocks go forward. What does that mean?"

"The clocks go forward on Sunday at 1:00 a.m."

"So it's on Sunday."

"Exactly."

"Did they give any indication of a specific time?"

"No, just that it's on that day. But it will be when it's at its busiest, won't it?"

"Of course."

Jameson considered this.

"Right, so today's Friday, giving us two days," he said. "This is what we do — we go to Brighton and we—"

"I think I should go see Sullivan."

"What? Why?"

"So he knows what we've found and can alert us of any erratic behaviour from Azeer."

It was as good of an excuse as any.

"Fine. While you do that, I'll get people to Brighton Pier."

"Evacuate?"

"No. There's going to be another attack, and if we evacuate now, they'll just change it to a new location." He put his hands in his pockets, looked out the window, and contemplated. "We need to station people at Brighton Pier — not our team, we can't trust them; we'll go, and we'll handpick some police officers we've worked with before to be on standby, officers we trust. Someone is bound to check the location before they attack, aren't they? So we watch. We spend today and Saturday on the Pier, a covert operation, looking for any known Alhami supporters, any deliberately inconspicuous behaviour, anyone looking out of place, anything — have firearms on standby. I'll get in touch with agents already performing surveillance on Alhami members, especially those in Brighton. Whatever we do, we need to be discreet. We can't let them know that we know."

"And if we don't catch them before Sunday?"

"Then we close the pier and arrest anyone we suspect."

"Is it a good idea to just go around arresting anyone we suspect? It would look pretty awful to have a police van full of innocent Muslims."

"Are you saying we should prioritise race relations over saving hundreds of lives?"

Kelly raised her eyebrows.

"All right, I get what you're saying," he said. "Look — you did well, Kelly. Really well. I'll get a team and we'll go through procedure. You go speak to Sullivan then we'll reconvene in Brighton in four hours. I'll let you know when we have a safe house."

"Sounds like a plan."

He rushed out of the room.

She finished translating the last few minutes of recording, then booked herself a taxi to HMP Brenthall, wondering whether Sullivan would even care if she showed up or not.

CHAPTER TWENTY-FOUR

Sullivan emerged into the courtyard with the rest of E Wing. Azeer's group sat on their bench, being rowdy like normal, but they didn't interfere with Sullivan, nor did they look in his direction.

Sullivan wandered around the courtyard, killing time, stretching, walking the perimeter. There was little to do, but he needed the fresh air. Being in his cell for 23 hours a day was getting boring, so it was nice to be bored outside instead.

After half an hour or so of aimless walking, Azeer and his group caught Sullivan's attention.

A man sat at a bench. Probably in his seventies, maybe his eighties. On his own. Sullivan was sure he'd heard a screw call him Al. He had a pack of cards in front of him, playing what looked like Solitaire.

Sullivan saw Azeer's head turning toward this man before his group did. Azeer nodded in Al's direction, and the rest of the group turned and laughed.

"Boy's playing Solitaire," he heard one of them say between sniggers.

Sullivan wondered what was so hilarious about a man

occupying his time inside with a game or two of Solitaire. But, to Azeer's group, this seemed like a perfect opportunity to show off to everyone just what a bunch of dicks they were.

They approached Al and said something to him. One of them brushed Al's cards aside, knocking most of them to the floor.

Al didn't say anything. He dropped his head, more in annoyance than fear, and avoided looking any of them in the eyes.

One of them grabbed the back of his hair, and shoved his head into his cards.

Sullivan sighed.

He should not get involved.

He should stay out of trouble.

Avoid drawing attention to himself.

Yet, even as he told himself this, he found his legs marching forward, and before he knew it, he was at Al's side.

He did not speak to Azeer, nor did he even acknowledge the group's presence. Instead, he crouched down and picked Al's cards up for him.

"Look at him," said one of them.

"He's got brains, this one!" said another.

Once Sullivan had picked up every last card, he placed them back in front of Al.

Hasim went to swipe them away again, but Sullivan grabbed Hasim's wrist before he managed.

Now, now, he told himself. *No drawing attention to yourself. No creating a scene.*

He let the wrist go.

"I saw you on the news," Hasim said. "You think you're a big man, don't you?"

Al looked up at Sullivan, as if to ask him what he thought he was doing.

Sullivan looked around for one of the screws. They didn't

even care. In fact, they were more preoccupied with checking the time and ensuring the prisoners didn't stay outside for a minute more than they were allowed.

"You think you're safe in here?" Azeer asked, his voice low and hushed. "You're not safe anywhere from me."

The whistle interrupted them, and they all began to return to their cells.

Al took his cards and shuffled past Sullivan without lifting his head.

Sullivan sighed, wondered why he did these things, and returned to his cell.

Just as he'd finished his piss, turned the news on, and settled on his bed, he heard some shuffling from outside his door.

It unlocked.

Then nothing.

He watched the door, waiting for one of the screws to come in, but they didn't.

After a few minutes, however, the door did open. Only a prison officer did not stand there.

Azeer did. As did Hasim. As did the rest of them.

Sullivan sighed. He wondered how much they had paid the screw for this.

They entered his cell. Closed the door. Stood over him, saying nothing.

They must think they look really scary, Sullivan thought.

But they were nothing. He could have them all squealing on the floor, clutching their broken bones, begging for mercy, and he could do it in less than a minute.

He stood, ready to fight.

Then he remembered — *no attracting unnecessary attention.*

Imagine he beat the shit out of them — what then?

He didn't have the screws in his pocket like they did. He didn't have access to his money from inside even if he did want to bribe them. An altercation where he left in the better state would mean he'd be moved cells for sure.

What's more, if they were all in hospital, there would be no way for him to record their conversations. Many, many people would die.

No, he could not break their bones or force them to beg for mercy.

He could do nothing but take the beating.

He took in a deep breath, held it, then let it out.

He relaxed his body.

Closed his eyes.

"Come on then, boys," he said. "Do your worst."

The first fist that landed was in his stomach. The second was on the back of his head. The next was a kick that took his ankles out.

He lay on the floor, covered his head, and took the beating.

The pain he could take — that was nothing.

The real torture was the humiliation of being beaten by a cretin such as Azeer Nadeem.

He promised himself he'd get him.

Once this was over, he'd get him.

And Sullivan would give a far better beating than this group of thugs could ever manage.

CHAPTER TWENTY-FIVE

An hour or so later, one of the older, female screws unlocked his cell door and barked, "You have a visitor."

Sullivan left his cell and wondered if she was the one who had unlocked the door so he could take his beating. He followed her off E Wing, through a corridor, and into a visitor room, where he found Kelly waiting.

"You have half an hour," the screw said, and shut the door, with no idea she was talking to a member of MI5.

Kelly stood, as if she was about to run up to Sullivan but paused, her hands covering her mouth as she gasped.

From the look of horror on her face, Sullivan imagined the wounds left by Azeer's gang were pretty bad.

"You should see the other guy," he said, limping in and sitting beside Kelly, who remained standing and staring, as if the shock was such that she did not know what to do.

He rubbed his ribs. He was sure they must be bruised. That, and the feeling that his nose was clogged up with dried blood, that his cheekbones were still throbbing, and that he couldn't move his leg without his thigh being in agony, meant that he couldn't get comfortable — which was probably the most frustrating part of it all.

Kelly finally sat and put her hand on his knee. The gesture was not reciprocated.

Still, she left the hand there.

"You didn't bring me any water or anything?"

She snapped herself out of her shock and said, "Oh yeah," then passed a bottle of water to Sullivan.

"I've been fucking killing for a clean bottle of water," he said as he screwed off the top, then downed half of it. "Almost as much as I've been killing for a whiskey."

"How did this happen, Jay?"

"What, me being thirsty?"

"You know damn well what I mean."

"Yeah, I do."

He took another swig.

"Well?" she prompted.

"Azeer Nadeem and his boys jumped me."

"What?"

"Couldn't hardly fight back, could I? Didn't want to be known as the difficult guy who can't take a beating."

"Well do they know what you're doing?"

"No."

"Then why on earth would they give you such a beating?"

Sullivan shrugged.

"If they have any suspicions, any at all, then we need to—"

"Relax, relax. They don't know shit. I provoked them, that is all."

"You provoked them?"

"That's what I said."

"I thought you were meant to be keeping your head down! You were meant to be unnoticed."

"What, are you my mum now?"

"Stop it, Jay. I'm being serious. If you can't handle this—"

"You have no fucking idea what I can handle."

He finished the bottle then crushed it in his hand.

"This is what you came here for?" he said. "To chastise me?"

He dabbed a cut on his forehead. It left blood on his fingers.

"No. No, I didn't."

"Then what did you come for?"

She hesitated.

"Because I missed you," she said.

"You missed me?"

"Yes. And I also wanted you to know we've translated what you've recorded. We have the date and time of the next attack."

Sullivan's eyes widened. "Where? When?"

Kelly lowered her voice.

"Brighton Pier. They said it would be on the day of the night the clocks go forward. The clocks go forward on Sunday morning, so we have two days."

"Two days?"

"After I've finished here, I'm going to join a team in Brighton. We're going to be staking out the pier over the next two days. We have a list of people who we think—"

"I don't need to know what your strategy is."

Just as Alexander had taught him. He was a soldier — he pulled the trigger, and left the strategies to the people who give the orders. As far as he was concerned, he could do nothing to help in Brighton, so understanding their strategy wouldn't help him.

Still, he was slightly worried, however much he didn't want to admit it. Kelly was going to be at the location of the attack. What if the intel was wrong? What if she had mistranslated? What if she got hurt?

No. She could take care of herself. She didn't need his concern.

He decided, nevertheless, to just say, "Be careful," before standing up and getting ready to return to his cell.

"Is that it?" Kelly objected, standing up also.

"What?"

"You're just going?"

"You need to get to Brighton. I don't want to hold you up."

"Jay, why are you like this? You don't need to be so stand-offish. You don't—"

She stopped talking. Stepped forward. Placed a delicate hand on his bruised cheek, and placed a light kiss on his lips, then a more passionate one.

They heard a tap on the window. Sullivan looked over his shoulder to see the screw telling them to knock it off.

He took a step away from Kelly.

"I will call you on Sunday evening at 9:00 p.m. to update you," she told him.

"Okay," he said. "Good luck."

"Is that it?"

"They said there will also be a third attack. I still need to—"

"That's not what I meant."

He looked at her.

She was a fierce woman. She was everything a weak man would fear and a strong man would want.

He had no idea which category he fell into.

"I love you, Jay," she said.

"Don't," he said. "Please, just... don't."

He turned. Walked away. Re-entered the prison corridor that led back to his cell, and did not look back.

Kelly needed to love someone who was good enough for her, and that would never be him.

STOKE-ON-TRENT, UNITED KINGDOM

FIVE YEARS AGO

CHAPTER TWENTY-SIX

Zain had never felt secure — not in his body, his mind, nor in the world. He had always kept himself to himself at school, and he rarely interacted with anyone at the mosque. Yet, the more time he spent with Azeer, the more confident he felt. Zain could just listen to his friend for hours and never notice a minute passing by.

As his eighteenth birthday approached, Azeer could see Zain was feeling a little down. He'd spoken to his parents on the phone — they'd had little to say to each other, and he'd ended the conversation quickly. Therefore, Azeer insisted that they would go out that evening and take his mind off it.

And so they spent another evening talking about all the things Azeer believed in.

"See, the West wrote their history books, didn't they?" Azeer said as he eyeballed some guy who was staring at him across the restaurant. "So whatever you read is written from the way they look at it."

Zain decided this was the best opportunity to ask a question he'd been wondering for a while.

"But some things are difficult for them to skew."

"Like what? You tell me one thing that you have been taught and I will tell you why it's wrong."

"Okay, how about the Gulf War?"

"What about it?"

"I mean, Saddam Hussain invaded another country. He killed people."

"And you think that's why America and the UK intervened?"

"Yes."

"No, Zain. You're getting their side, and their side only, aren't you? Yes, Saddam invaded Kuwait, but countries invade other countries all the time, why were the United Nations so bothered this time?"

"I don't know."

"I'll tell you why. Because it was Islam they were fighting against, not Saddam."

"What do you mean?"

"The West wants to stop the spread of Islam. They do not want the number of Islamic countries to grow, do you understand? They went to war because they figured one less Muslim country is one less problem." In almost the same breath, Azeer looked at the guy who was still staring at him. "What the fuck are you looking at?"

The guy looked around.

"Yes, I'm talking to you. You keep staring at me. What do you want?"

"I wasn't—"

"There must be a reason. What is it?"

"What?"

"You heard me. Stop staring."

The man stood up, shifting nervously, and left.

Zain marvelled at Azeer, caught between disbelief and admiration. The way he handled people like that...

Zain spent most of his time walking from one place to the

next with his head down and avoiding eye contact. The kind of people who once stabbed Fahad still existed. They still followed him, taunted him, and threatened him, and he was often scared to walk from one side of the town to the other.

"How are you so confident?" Zain asked. "People stare at me like that all the time and I don't do shit."

Azeer grinned. "They are scared of us. They think we are all terrorists."

"What?"

"After 9/11, they look at us and assume that we all have bombs strapped to our chest. If we tell them to back off, they get scared about what we might do."

Zain mulled this over. Did they really think that? Did they look at him and assume he was a terrorist?

"I'll tell you what you should do," Azeer continued, "next time they stare at you or cause trouble — you tell them you are a suicide bomber and you have explosives strapped to your chest."

"And they will believe me?"

"Trust me. That's how convinced they are that we're all part of Al Qaeda."

The next day, with Azeer's assertions ringing around his mind, he walked through town with a newfound sense of confidence. When those looks were aimed at him, instead of avoiding them, this time he looked back. He let them think he was the murderer they thought he was. He let their racist inclinations create their own fear.

"Yo, paki boy," he heard one person say. "Get out of our country."

Normally, Zain would speed up his walking and get out of there quickly.

On this particular day, he stopped. Turned toward the man standing outside some cheap clothes store, his group of mates stood around him.

"What did you just say?" Zain asked.

"You heard me."

The man stepped closer.

Zain did not move.

"You want some, do you?" the man said. "You want us to get you out of our country?"

Zain studied this man. His cockiness, the way he strutted, the way his friends encouraged him — in a way, Zain wished he did actually have a bomb on him. He wished he could blow this guy up.

"I got a bomb on me," he said.

"What?" The man laughed with his mates.

Zain looked beneath his jacket and pretended to move something; pretended to readjust his bomb vest.

"I am a suicide bomber and I have a bomb on me." He stepped toward the man, who stepped back. "You want me to burn you up?"

The man looked to his mates. His face changed. He was actually believing this.

How was he so stupid to actually believe that Zain was just casually walking around town with a bomb strapped to him? Did this man actually believe that anyone who was part of Islam just got up in the morning, put on their vest of explosives, and went about their day?

"Yeah, we're sorry," the man said. "We're cool. We're fine. We didn't mean it, yeah?"

The fear in the man's eyes was real.

It was the fear Zain had seen in his own reflection so many times.

He couldn't quite believe it was that easy. That they believed in their paranoia so deeply, and that they were either that thick, or that racist.

Azeer was right.

These people did deserve to die.

HMP BRENTHALL, UNITED KINGDOM

NOW

CHAPTER TWENTY-SEVEN

It was Saturday afternoon, and Sullivan felt a little nervous. He had no idea how well Kelly and Jameson were doing, whether their team had made any arrests, or even made progress in monitoring the situation.

They had until tomorrow to catch the attackers. Then what? What if they didn't?

It was a no-win situation. If they evacuate the pier, they won't catch the terrorist, and Alhami will just attack somewhere else. But if they don't evacuate the pier, and they don't manage to catch the terrorist — people die and they could have prevented it.

He walked through the courtyard with a small limp, and bruises and scabs on his face. Azeer and his group looked over and allowed themselves a little chuckle. They thought they'd broken his spirit.

Little did they know, his spirit had already been broken a long time ago.

He sat on a bench. Looked around. He had nothing to do, and he was bored.

That's when he noticed Al approaching, using his walking

stick to help him over. He stopped beside Sullivan and held his hand out.

"My name is Alan," he said. "You can call me Al."

Sullivan shook his hand. He was so used to not telling anyone his name that he almost forgot it had already been broadcast all over the news almost two weeks ago.

"Jay," he said.

"Mind if I sit?"

"Depends. You got those cards with you?"

"I have."

"Know how to play Rummy?"

"Sure do."

"Then take a seat."

Al sat down, leant his walking stick against the bench, and took out his pack of cards. He dealt, and they engaged in a game of Rummy.

After a few rounds, Al spoke.

"I wanted to thank you," he said. "What you did was foolish and unnecessary, but it took guts to do it. And, by the look of it, you've paid the price."

"I've taken a beating before."

"I'm sure you have." Al paused. "I saw you on the news. You're that assassin, aren't you?"

"Ex-assassin."

"Used to work for the government?"

"That's how it started."

"So why did you let them beat you?"

"What?"

This stumped Sullivan. He wasn't expecting this question.

"Why did you let Azeer and his gang of idiots beat you? Surely you'd have been taught how to take on a bunch of guys like that."

Sullivan shrugged. He wasn't sure what to say and wanted

to change the conversation quickly, so he said the first thing that came to mind.

"Hey, the clocks are changing — is this the one where we gain an hour, or lose an hour?"

"We lose it."

"And it's tomorrow, yeah? The day of the night the clocks go forward?"

"Well, if you want to get technical, that's tonight."

Sullivan froze.

"What?" he said.

"Well, the clocks change at 1:00 a.m. — which is tomorrow morning, or today's tonight. So, technically, tomorrow is the day of the *morning* the night goes back, and today is the day of the *night* the clock goes back."

Sullivan took a moment for that to sink in.

Al was right.

Tomorrow was not the night of the clocks going back.

That was *today*.

How had they been so stupid?

No, they couldn't be wrong. Kelly and Jameson were smart. It was a technicality. It was just the way it was phrased, that was all. The attack had to be tomorrow, not today.

Yet, as much as he told himself this, he didn't believe it.

He suddenly realised how things could be about to go so very wrong.

"Shit," he said and, without any explanation to Al, he leapt from his seat, sprinting through the courtyard and back into the cells.

He already knew he would be too late.

He was trapped in prison, and there was little he could do.

BRIGHTON PIER, UNITED KINGDOM

CHAPTER TWENTY-EIGHT

Abdul drove his car along Marine Parade, pulled into a street called New Steine, and parked his car.

The car parking charge was extortionate but, just as he went to pay it, he remembered — he didn't need to.

He was not going to be around to pay any parking tickets he might acquire.

He killed the engine. Put his hands on his knees. Breathed.

Just as Azeer had told him on the phone, he needed to breathe. He needed to take a moment. Ground himself. Think through it. Calm his nerves.

Although he wasn't entirely certain whether it was nerves, or whether it was excitement.

This was the moment he'd waited for his whole life. His parents were proud. His comrades were proud.

Azeer was proud.

This was the greatest honour that could be bestowed upon anyone, and soon he would be with Allah.

He took off his t-shirt.

Pulled the box out from beneath the passenger seat.

Opened it.

There it was. The vest. Detonator attached. Enough explosives to send a clear message to all of those who wish to stop the spread of Islam.

At first, he just held the vest. Closed his eyes. Ran his fingers over it. Felt the bumps of the various bombs. Felt the beauty of its imminent destruction.

He put the vest on.

Put his t-shirt back on.

And put his coat on.

He stepped out of the car and locked it — again, wondering why he was bothering to lock it. It wasn't as if he'd be bothered should someone steal it.

He crossed the road and walked along Marine Parade. The beach was to his left, and it was full of happy families. For early spring, it was pleasantly hot, and families were spending this weekend relishing the little time they had to enjoy the beach in such nice weather. The winter had been long and cold but it finally felt like it was over, and the children were collecting pebbles and paddling in the sea and throwing frisbees and they all looked so happy.

He walked past the Sea Life Centre he'd taken his little brother to when they were younger and crossed a roundabout.

As he approached the pier, a few stalls and food vans with pleasant aromas greeted him. There was coffee, cake, hot dogs, candy floss, crepes, and he felt hungry.

A small makeshift train went past him, full of tourists about to be driven down the pier and back. Seagulls called out above; the soundtrack to any seaside. He could barely move for people. They knocked into him, and even apologised on occasion.

He walked further into the pier. The lit-up sign of *Brighton*

Pier welcomed him forward, along with hordes of families, people in swimsuits, and couples with ice creams.

He was suddenly nervous. His forehead perspired. He tried to be confident, but he felt sick.

Something made him turn around. He wasn't sure why; it was instinctive. Like someone was watching him.

Something felt wrong.

On the road beside the pier, he saw them.

A black van parked discreetly, but not discreet enough; it was parked too perfectly, like its driver was trying to appear inconspicuous. Abdul watched the van for a few seconds, long enough to see a glimpse of a firearms police officer open and close the backdoor.

They knew.

They were here.

He peered up and down the pier. They must have noticed him by now.

He took a deep breath.

Put his finger on the detonator.

"Abdul, wait!" shouted a woman's voice.

He looked over his shoulder at a woman rushing toward him.

There was no reason to wait any longer.

CHAPTER TWENTY-NINE

Kelly had seen him walking warily onto the pier, looking around. He seemed too cautious, too contemplative. He was looking everywhere, sweating, his facial expression both strong and weak, his body language hunched with a nervous determination.

Her instincts screamed at her that something was wrong about this man. She did not trust him.

She stepped away from her bench, put down the newspaper she had been pretending to read, and followed him. It was busy and she struggled to keep sight of him, even at only twenty or so yards away. She had to barge past a few people and ignore a few complaints — but, should she save their lives, she was sure they would let her off a gentle nudge.

"Clay Ten," she said, using Jameson's code name, knowing her hidden mic would pick her up. "Look at the man entering the pier now. Short, wearing a coat."

"Roger, Zero Two, I see him," Jameson's voice said in her ear. He was further along the pier, watching.

"Do we know him?"

"Hang on, we're checking."

As Kelly waited for intel, she continued to trail him.

He was looking around at everything. The food stands, the families, the signs. His eyes were wide. His hand was clutching something in his pocket.

Was he the one who'd be committing the act tomorrow?

She managed to find a small gap in the crowds and stared harder at his pocket. What was he holding? It was like a phone, but slightly bigger.

His thumb traced something over it...

"Zero Two this is Clay Ten," said Jameson. "Target's name is Abdul Hasar. He has connections to members of Alhami."

"He has something in his hand."

"What?"

"It looks like a detonator."

"It could be a phone."

"It's not a phone."

A moment's silence responded

"I'll make the arrest," Kelly decided. "Zero Two moving in. Where are the firearms?"

"Standby, Zero Two."

"What?"

"Stand down, wait for confirmation."

"What confirmation?"

No answer.

"What is it?" she tried again.

Another pause.

"His jacket is too thick," Jameson said. "He looks like he's wearing a vest."

Kelly followed the target further onto the pier. Jameson was right. His jacket was too thick.

"The attack is tomorrow, isn't it?"

Jameson didn't answer.

"Clay Ten, please confirm."

"Get off the pier, Zero Two. Get everyone off the pier."

"It's too late for that, they won't have time; I have to stop him."

"Don't be a fucking hero, Kelly. Evacuate."

"The first sign of evacuation and he'll detonate."

"Kelly—"

"I have no choice. I'm going to try and stall him — tell the firearms to wait. Once I have my hand on the detonator, take him out."

The firearms unit readied themselves and approached the pier's entrance. They could be there in thirty seconds.

But, just as she saw the target's hand leave his jacket, she knew thirty seconds would be too long.

He was about to hit the trigger.

CHAPTER THIRTY

"Abdul, wait!" she shouted.

He stopped walking. Turned. Stared at her.

"Abdul, my name is Kelly, I—"

"I don't care who you are."

"You don't have to do this."

Abdul saw the firearms in the distance, approaching the pier.

"Clay Ten, he can see the firearms, tell them to hold," she told Jameson over the radio. The last thing she wanted was to spook a terrorist with an itchy trigger finger, or inspire panic from civilians. Plus, she didn't know what kind of detonator the target was holding — he could be holding a button down that, when released, set off the bomb; which meant shooting him would be the worst thing they could do.

"Abdul," she said, edging closer to him. "Please. We are not who you think we are."

She knew that saying such a thing to a man who had been deeply radicalised wouldn't change his mind — but she didn't know what else to say. Was she supposed to beg? Plead? Convince him that it was wrong?

"Abdul, many people will die. They don't need to."

He said nothing.

He turned back to the pier.

"Abdul, please."

Abdul flexed his fingers around the detonator.

He shouted, "Allahu Akbar!" then ran further onto the pier.

"Shit," said Kelly.

She looked around frantically at the children with their buckets and the mums with their coffees and the dads with their ice creams and the old couples holding hands and the people having fun with no idea what was about to happen — and she did the only thing she could.

"Everyone get off the pier!"

No one paid attention.

She shouted louder.

"I am MI5, everyone get off the pier now!"

A few faces glanced in her direction.

"There is a bomb! Evacuate! There is a terrorist threat, get off the pier now!"

Just as she shouted it, the firearms officers came rushing past.

Now they paid attention. The pier shook under the stampede of feet running for their dear lives.

Kelly knew it would do no good, but if she could get them off the pier, then that meant the firearms units could take their shot without anyone in the way. They could do so with minimal casualties.

She knew this was just wishful thinking.

The target ran into the nearest building where holidaymakers played on the slots, putting two penny pieces into machines to push out prizes, going through the house of horrors, playing table hockey — all completely unaware.

She thought, *how did we get this wrong?*

"Kelly!" she heard a voice shout from behind her.

It was Jameson.

He was evacuating the pier.

"Kelly, come on!" he insisted, shouting to be heard above the mass of souls fleeing for their lives.

She knew there was no point. There was no way she could get far enough away from the blast in time. Instead, she ran to the pier's edge and looked at the sea below.

She climbed onto the ledge and hesitated.

It was a big drop. The water was deep. But it was her only option.

She closed her eyes, took a breath, and jumped.

As she fell, she thought of her mum and wondered how MI5 would break the news of her death.

She thought of her job, and wondered how they managed to screw up two attacks so close to each other.

She thought of Sullivan. A troubled man, but one she loved.

The blast was loud and left a ringing in her ears.

She hit the water's surface and her thoughts ended as she lost consciousness.

The explosion destroyed the pier, which collapsed on the beach. Jameson, still shouting for his partner, was killed instantly.

Kelly's lifeless body sunk lower and lower as the rumble of the pier preceded its collapse.

HMP BRENTHALL, UNITED KINGDOM

CHAPTER THIRTY-ONE

SULLIVAN DID NOT CARE WHO HE BARGED OUT OF THE WAY to get inside — whether it was a screw, an inmate, a psycho, whatever. He'd managed to fade into the background and remain unnoticed by most inmates, but in that moment he did not care who he pissed off. He didn't even bother going back to his cell — he stopped in the communal area where the television was already on, and both screws and inmates were watching the news.

"We are getting more reports about the explosion on Brighton Pier," said the news reporter. "Early reports have confirmed that it was a terrorist attack, although no official statement has been made, and we will update you on this as we find out more. What we do know, however, is that most of the pier has collapsed. Many tourists both on the pier, and on the beach below, have been caught in its destruction."

The report cut to an aerial image taken by a helicopter as it hovered over the scene. The end of the pier was a pile of rubble and flames on the beach below. Firefighters were still tackling the blaze, and paramedics were doing what they could to revive the bodies scattered around the pier's entrance.

"Whether this is linked to the terrorist attack of Camden Market two weeks ago, has yet to be confirmed, and we are still waiting for comment from Downing Street."

At first, Sullivan couldn't believe it. It was surreal. Like he was underwater, and all the voices were unclear.

He had recorded the conversation.

Kelly had translated it.

It was going to be tomorrow; they were sure of it.

Except they were wrong.

Kelly...

Was she alive?

She said she was going to be there, staking out the pier... had she survived?

He rushed to the phone. He hadn't called her so far, not wanting anyone to make a link between him and an MI5 agent, but in this moment he didn't care. Clear thinking wasn't an option. Even if he just heard her voice, just heard her say hello, then he could hang up, knowing she was alive.

He fumbled over the numbers and, in his commotion, got her number wrong and had to redial.

He put the phone to his ear.

Listened.

Ringing, and ringing, and more ringing, and even more ringing, until, "Hi, I can't reach the phone right now, but if you would like to leave a message—"

"Shit," Sullivan barked, slamming the phone back on the receiver.

This could mean nothing.

If she was alive, she was probably in the midst of helping people. The last thing she would think to do was let him know she was okay, especially after how their last exchange went.

She could still be alive.

She could be.

He bowed his head. He was kidding himself. He'd been around death for long enough to know that misguided hope never came to anything.

So what could he do?

He could fight his way out of the prison and try to find her. He may or may not manage to get out, but what then?

The whole operation would be blown.

There was still going to be another attack. An even bigger one. If he left, he wouldn't be able to record Azeer's conversations. If he tried to leave and failed, he'd be moved to solitary confinement. Many, many more lives would die just so he could find out if Kelly was alive.

But he had to know.

Then he thought — Kelly had said that she would call him at 9:00 p.m. on Sunday evening. If she was alive, then she would call.

If she wasn't alive...

So he'd have to get through the night, not knowing.

He could do that.

Right?

It dawned on him that he didn't know if Jameson was alive, either — as, if they were both dead, there would be no one to get him out of prison. He would be stuck inside, probably for the rest of his life, and unable to do anything about the imminent attack.

So much rested on one phone call.

He would not be able to get much sleep, he knew that. But he didn't need it. He was used to surviving on little sleep. As an assassin, he was trained to deal with all kinds of conditions.

But he had never been trained in what to do when faced with losing someone he cared about.

He'd lost his wife to murder.

He'd lost his daughter — albeit, not to murder, but to a different path. He wondered if Talia had seen him on the news, had seen he was captured, and he wondered if she would be pleased or sad.

Or if she would care at all.

He wanted to punch something. The wall, a face, whatever — he needed to release his fury.

His arms were shaking, and he did not know whether that was from alcohol withdrawal or anger.

"We are now receiving confirmation from the government that Alhami, the terrorist cell who committed the attacks of Camden Market, are also claiming responsibility for this attack. The Prime Minister is due to give a press conference in the next hour where he warns the public of even more attacks to come."

Sullivan turned to enter his cell.

As he did, he saw him. Azeer. Standing outside his cell, watching the television over everyone's shoulders.

Sullivan had never seen a man look so smug, and was desperate to beat the look off his face.

But he had to stop the next attack. He had to keep his rage inside. Had to bury his feelings deep, deep down.

For now.

As soon as he was able, he would see to that smug face.

He swore on the life of his estranged daughter that, when the day came, he would make sure Azeer suffered.

CHAPTER THIRTY-TWO

That night was the slowest night yet.

He'd forced himself to remain apathetic to everyone he met for so long, and now he didn't know how to handle caring about someone. He'd told Kelly numerous times that she was nothing to him, that it would never be a relationship, that it was only fucking — yet she was all he could think about. Occasionally he would drift into a light sleep, just so he could wake up again and turn to see if she was there.

But she was never there.

And he had no idea if she would ever be in a bed next to him again.

"Stop it," he growled to himself and rubbed his eyes.

Eventually, the early morning haze appeared outside the small window in his cell, and he gave up trying to sleep. Sunrise was close, and there was little point continuing his attempt at sleeping.

He stood up. Stretched his back. Filled the kettle. Put it on and found his only sachet of coffee. They weren't particularly liberal with how much coffee prisoners were allowed.

This was because of a druggy who ran out of coke and started snorting coffee instead, only to choke on the granules.

Even coffee granules were deemed too dangerous for these bloody cretins.

He contemplated whether to turn on the television. Did he really want to hear more about how much devastation there was?

Then again, he needed to know what was happening.

He turned on the television. Sipped on his coffee as he watched a smartly dressed man speak.

"The current death toll is standing at 107 — but, again, this does not count for the hundreds missing or in intensive—"

He turned the television off again.

He was wrong. He didn't need to know what was happening.

He spent the hour before breakfast exercising to pass the time, trying to ignore how much his arms shook. He thought he'd be over the alcohol withdrawal by now, but it still persisted, every morning without fail, the sweats and the pains and the aches. He tried a few push ups and a few press ups, but it was a stupid idea.

All he could think about was Kelly.

Breakfast came and he queued up for the standard spoonful of crap. Azeer stood further along the queue, a few people between them, and Sullivan tried not to stare but it was all he could do. Even the back of his head looked arrogant, with the folds of his neck beneath the close shave of his hair.

Sullivan noticed a fork in his hand, and he couldn't help imagining all the ways he could use that fork to end Azeer's life.

Putting it down his throat and choking him on it.

Press the prongs against his throat until blood seeped past it.

Force it up Azeer's nostrils and cover his mouth.

All these ways, yet he didn't do one of them. He just collected his shitty breakfast and ate what he could of it before he needed to be sick, then passed the next few hours in his cell.

The afternoon hour came, where the screw would unlock their cells, and let them roam for sixty minutes — or less if the screw was bored or if there was some trouble to contend with.

He fell into the crowd shuffling into the courtyard, and kept himself to himself. He did a bit of exercise, trying to kill the monotony, trying to keep his mind occupied.

Then he returned to his cell and watched the news for the next six hours. It was the same headlines over and over again, only a larger number of deaths were reported each time.

Six o'clock in the evening came. As did seven, as did eight...

In the hour approaching nine, he grew nervous. A strange kind of nervousness, where he kept needing to throw up, only to find he couldn't.

Fifty minutes to go. Forty, thirty...

He turned off the news. He'd had enough.

He paced back and forth. His muscles ached, but he could no longer stay still.

Twenty, ten...

He closed his eyes. Placed his forehead against the wall. Told himself to stop being a wreck, to get a grip. It was just a woman.

He snorted.

Evidently, this was not just a woman, and he regretted not telling her that. In fact, he decided that, when she called, he would get over himself and tell her how he really felt.

Which she was going to do.

She was going to call. There was no doubt about it. She would.

Because she was a smart woman; far more intelligent than he was. She would survive.

Eight, seven, six...

He wiped sweat from his forehead. Bit his lip. Went to punch the wall, then didn't, not understanding where the urge had come from.

Five, four, three...

He huffed. Sighed. Held his breath, looking to the ceiling, as if there would be an answer from some divine being he did not believe in.

Two, one...

He stood by the small window in his cell door.

Zero.

He readied himself to leave, expecting a screw to come along and tell him he had a phone call.

But no one came.

Another minute passed, then another, then another.

And still, no one came.

He told himself not to think anything bad just yet. These screws were crap. Often, mail wouldn't arrive until a week after the prison had received it. People were taken late to their visitations. Information was not passed on. They were hardly efficient, and he convinced himself that it was the screw's inability to perform even the most menial task that was the issue.

However, as the minutes passed and passed, it became more and more difficult to convince himself of this.

As another hour came and went, then another, and the darkness of night grew thicker, he found it more and more difficult to rationalise any way that Kelly could still be alive, and denial grew more and more difficult.

Maybe she'd forgotten?

Which was ridiculous, of course. Kelly never forgot anything. She was always true to her word.

He tried to keep his shit together. He tried to hold in his anger. He hated feeling so helpless.

He cursed every woman who had ever given him affection. Why did he do it? Why did he get involved with Kelly when he knew that any woman who fell for him died?

He wanted a drink.

No, he needed a drink.

He stood up. Had to get off his knees.

How would he complete the mission without Kelly?

He didn't know Arabic.

He only had one recorder with limited capacity.

Kelly was the smart one. Sullivan knew how to beat a man to death, how to murder a target with a tie, how to kill a person without anyone knowing how they had been killed — but he did not know how to gather intelligence.

As the early hours of the morning arrived, Sullivan finally came to accept it — no one was coming to collect him for his phone call.

Kelly was dead.

As was Jameson.

And that also meant that the only people who knew of his operation were gone.

There would be no one coming to release him in two weeks, when those thirty days were up.

And there would be no way he could stop an attack from inside a cell.

Once again, he found himself alone.

Completely, utterly, and unquestionably alone.

BRIGHTON BEACH

CHAPTER THIRTY-THREE

Kelly wasn't quite sure what was happening.

She wasn't even sure if she was alive.

She was wet, she could tell that. Everything was blurry, but blue, like a bright sky was above her.

Orange blurs flickered too. Was that fire?

There was screaming. Lots of it. Sirens. It was too much.

And she was being dragged.

Who was dragging her?

The ground was rough, bumpy like rocks.

Her clothes were heavy. Drenched.

Her head rolled to the side. Her eyes closed and opened a while later.

"Jay?"

She was dragged onto harder ground. Was this gravel?

"Jay, is that you?"

It wasn't. She knew that.

Didn't she?

Her thoughts weren't quite making sense.

Why was there so much noise, and why was it so far away?

She choked. Water dribbled down her chin.

"Jay…"

She was lifted into something. Hands grabbed her. She was dumped on a solid floor. Some doors closed and the bright blue was replaced by darkness.

Was this a van?

She groaned. Coughed up water.

Two hits on the side of the van and it took off.

She was rocking, like she was on a child's ride, or sitting on a washing machine.

She turned her head.

Someone was looking at her.

She couldn't see the face.

"Where's Jay…"

They shushed her.

Who the hell was he to shush her?

She did not accept this typical chauvinism you get in the workplace where men shush her and demean her and…

She wasn't in the workplace, though.

Was she?

No, it was a van.

She was pretty sure it was a van.

Jay was there.

No he wasn't.

It was another man.

"Don't you fucking…"

She tried to say *shush me* but it didn't come out. Her throat hurt when she spoke, and she coughed up more water.

Why were her clothes so heavy?

Because she was wet.

How did she get wet in a van?

Was she in a van?

Because she had been in the sea.

Why was she in the sea?

She turned over again. So many thoughts, so little sense.

She tried to push herself up but her arms gave way.

"Relax," a man said.

Relax?

He can't tell her to relax...

Who was he?

"Trust me," he said, his voice echoing like they were in a bathroom. "You are going to need your energy."

She didn't like that.

It sounded like a threat. Like the man was trying to intimidate her.

She pushed herself up again, but fell.

She closed her eyes.

Next thing she knew, she was being carried. She tried kicking and punching, but barely managed to flounce.

"Let me go..."

She was dumped on something. Her back hurt. Something cold clamped around her wrists.

"Jay, where are you..."

"Man hazih?"

"'Enaha ta'emal lada almukhabarat alaskariya."

She knew Arabic. She knew they were asking who she was. They knew she was MI5.

A few dirty looks and they left.

She tried to stand, but fell, partly due to her groggy state, partly due to her hands being held to the wall by chains.

She tried to pull, tried to free herself, tried to voice her objections.

It was useless. She was too weak. They had her.

CHAMAN, PAKISTAN, NEXT TO AFGHANISTAN BORDER

FOUR YEARS AGO

CHAPTER THIRTY-FOUR

Zain waited to be collected from outside the Government Degree College — a light yellow building surrounded by sand and dying grass. He found a tree and used it to shelter from the sun. It was hotter here than he could have imagined.

After a few hours, a car arrived. Azeer was in the passenger seat, and a man Zain didn't recognise was driving. He had a dark hat on, a large beard, and militant uniform.

"Get in," said Azeer.

Zain picked up his bag and climbed into the back.

"Hi," he said to the driver, offering his hand. "I'm Zain."

The driver did not turn to look at him.

"Sit down," said Azeer.

Zain sat down and put his seat belt on.

"Do not tell a stranger your name," Azeer said. "What are you thinking?"

"I just thought—"

"You are not allowed to know the general's names."

"Oh, I'm sorry."

"Put this on."

Azeer passed Zain a black hood.

Zain picked it up and looked back at Azeer, a little perplexed.

"Now," said Azeer.

Zain put the hood on.

For the next twenty minutes he could do nothing but listen to the rumble of the engine. It was not a smooth ride, and the car lifted off the ground on numerous occasions. Either they were on an extremely bumpy road, or they were not on a road at all.

The car eventually came to a stop.

"Can I take this off?" asked Zain.

The sound of car doors opening and closing was his response. A few seconds went by, and his door was opened.

"Keep it on," said Azeer's voice, and he felt Azeer's hand grip his arm and pull him out. The hand stayed on his arm as he was guided forward. His feet sunk a little bit and he could tell he was walking on sand.

He was brought into somewhere a little cooler — though, only a little, as it was still scorching.

Azeer took the hood off.

Zain looked around. He was in a large tent. In front of him, a man sat in a seat. Azeer took the seat next to him.

This new man scared him a little. He knew Azeer, and knew that the deadened expression he was wearing wasn't the real him, but he had no idea who this new guy was. He was staring at Zain with such a dismissive, unwelcoming look.

Zain stood awkwardly, waiting for them to talk.

"Min ayn 'ant?" the man said.

"What?"

"Min ayn 'ant?"

"I'm sorry, I don't speak—"

"Where are you from?" the man said instead, with a thick Pakistani accent.

"I, er — Southend."

"Where is that?"

"Essex. England."

"You were born there?"

"Yes, I was."

"And you lived there your whole life?"

"Yes, I did. Until a few years ago, when I moved to Stoke, mainly because—"

"And you have never left England?"

"No, I have not."

The man exchanged a look with Azeer.

"Then why do you want to betray your country?"

"What?"

The man raised his eyebrows. He was not about to repeat himself.

"I — well, I guess I don't really think of myself as having a country. My religion, and my brothers, they are more important than a country."

"Tell me about your religion and your brothers."

"Well, they, er — they are part of Islam. Part of a religion the country you say I'm part of wants to oppress."

"And why do you care?"

Zain went from being intimidated to mildly irritated. Who the hell did this guy think he was? He knew nothing of what Zain had been through.

"Because the country is made up of people who hate us."

"Is it?"

"Yes."

"And you are sure?"

"With all due respect, whoever you are, you did not see my friend Fahad die because of—"

The man raised his hand to indicate Zain to stop talking.

The man turned to Azeer. They had a quick conversation in Arabic, then the man turned back to Zain.

"Are you willing to fight?" the man asked.

"I have been fighting my whole—"

"Just a yes or no."

He paused, not sure whether to be annoyed or not. "Yes."

"And you are willing to kill people from your country?"

"Yes."

"And you are willing to die doing so?"

"Am I willing?"

The man raised his eyebrows.

"I am not only willing," Zain said. "But I am eager."

The man leant forward. "Why?"

"They have tried to stop the glory of Allah. They have killed anyone who wishes to spread the word of Islam, and it is time to send them a message."

"And what message is that?"

"That we will not be silenced."

"And you think you are the right person to do that?" Zain wasn't quite sure how to answer that. He glanced at Azeer, who was looking back at him with an intrigued smile, and he decided the best way to answer would be to repeat the words of the Quran that Azeer had taught him.

"Permission to take up arms is hereby given to those who are attacked because they have been oppressed. Allah indeed has the power to grant them victory."

The man finally smiled. He stood.

"Follow me," he said.

The man walked out of the tent. With a worried glance at Azeer, Zain followed. He emerged into the desert, passed a group of men combat training in perfect formation, and entered another tent.

The man opened the tent, let Zain walk in, then followed. He closed the tent and lit a few candles.

A man appeared in the flickers of amber. Caucasian male. Tied to a chair. Head dropped. So many bruises and wounds on his face that Zain was unable to tell what this guy had looked like before he was taken prisoner. Every breath came out in a croak, each exhalation another struggle.

"This is a United States Marine," Zain was told. "We captured him in Afghanistan three years ago."

Three years? thought Zain.

"We have learned all we can from him. He has since become redundant."

The man handed Zain a gun.

Zain stared at it.

"Take it," the man instructed.

Zain took the gun.

"Have you ever fired a gun before?"

"No."

He'd armed himself with knives, but never with guns. It was heavier than he thought it would be. He held it in his open palm and stared at it.

"Hold it properly."

Zain moved the gun so he held it like he'd seen in movies.

"This is a 9mm Glock. The ammunition is loaded. Point it at his head."

Zain lifted the gun, slowly, and pointed it at the prisoner's head.

"It's going to kickback, so put your hand beneath the grip to support it."

Zain placed his hand beneath the gun as instructed.

"Now kill the prisoner."

The words didn't quite sink in at first.

This wasn't what Zain was expecting.

He was imagining glory — fighting the opponent as they attacked him, or planting a bomb somewhere that would send a message.

He did not imagine he'd be killing an unarmed prisoner.

"This — this isn't what I thought it would—"

"What did you think it would be?" the man snapped.

"I thought I'd be returning fire. I didn't think I'd be killing an unarmed—"

"Do you want to stop their oppression? Do you want to be part of Alhami, part of the cause?"

"Yes I do."

"Then show me."

Zain knew he was going to have to do it. He knew he had no choice.

He thought of Fahad.

He thought of those murderers who stabbed him.

This man had probably killed many of his brothers for the same reasons.

He hated this man.

He built up the hatred, and he harnessed it into anger.

And he felt ready.

He aimed the gun and closed his eyes.

HMP BRENTHALL, UNITED KINGDOM

NOW

CHAPTER THIRTY-FIVE

"Do it," said Alexander.

Sullivan pointed his gun at the man.

Alexander had told him the man deserved it.

Unarmed prisoner or not, it was Sullivan's instructions and he needed to do as he was told.

"I'm waiting."

Sullivan closed his eyes and pulled the trigger.

He opened his eyes and quickly sat up. He was sweating. In his prison cell. The reverberation of the gunshot still ringing in his ears, despite it being a dream.

But it was not just a dream; it was a memory of the first man he'd ever killed. Alexander had trained him how to kill, then made him prove that he had the guts. He'd made Sullivan shoot a prisoner.

He'd explained that Sullivan couldn't always know the reasons why he was after a target; he would not be privy to their intelligence. All Sullivan needed to know was that, if he didn't kill the bad people, then those bad people would kill the good people.

Such an explanation made the task very simple.

After much coercion, Sullivan had done it.

He was just a kid. Years of abuse from his father and witnessing his mother's murder had taught him that causing pain was not only okay, but was as normal as pissing and shitting.

And Alexander had used that.

They used to have a tally on the wall. During their training, when rookies began to go into the field and commit their first hits, Alexander would record how many kills they'd executed and he would celebrate their milestones.

After ten, he'd shake your hand and pat you on the back.

After twenty, everyone would applaud you.

After thirty, you'd get your own house, and be considered for more dangerous hits. You'd become a professional, and you would be rewarded as such.

He remembered, though it was only fleeting, thinking how strange it was to celebrate the deaths of others. But Alexander likened it to any other job. If he sold cars, he would be rewarded for selling the most cars. If he were a teacher, he would celebrate his students getting the highest grades. If he was a politician, he would celebrate his election victory.

As an assassin, he celebrated his hits — as it meant he was performing his job well.

Sullivan remembered vividly, the day after his thirtieth hit, when Alexander declared that his training was over.

"Will I see you again?" Sullivan, just twenty-one years old, had asked.

"Do you wish to?"

"I don't know. It just feels weird. Three years, then suddenly nothing. Especially after all you've taught me."

"I have other recruits now, Jay. I have others who need to learn."

Sullivan looked down. It was strange, but he'd felt a little jealous. He'd enjoyed Alexander's attention. He had become a far stronger father figure than Sullivan's dad had been.

"You know you're different, don't you?" Alexander said.

"What?"

"I mean, yes, I train assassins, many of them competent. But you are in a different league."

"Are you being serious?"

"Yes, Jay. You have quite a talent. I imagine, in a few years' time, it will be you who teaches me things."

"Seriously?"

"Maybe you can come back and show the trainees a few things. Then we can catch up. Go for a drink."

Sullivan was proud of what Alexander had said to him, and remembered being disappointed that this was the end of his mentorship.

And now, standing at the sink of his prison cell, Sullivan could only look back at his younger self with pity. He may be locked up, but it was his younger self who had been imprisoned, desperately craving the approval from Alexander that he'd sought from his father.

He hadn't done the right thing then, nor had he done the right thing afterwards.

One doesn't just break out of years of brainwashing and conditioning and coercing.

Now he had the chance to do the right thing — but he could not do it from a prison cell. He had to find someone else at MI5. He had to tell them what had happened. He had to tell them who Azeer was, and he had to get them to find him another translator.

So he waited, just as he did the previous day, for the moment that afternoon when his cell would be unlocked.

He heard the cells across the corridor being unlocked first, and he waited by the door.

Ready.

Anticipating the moment.

As soon as his cell door opened, he swung his fist into the screw's face. They fell to the floor, not quite knocked out, but close to it.

He took their keys and ran.

He didn't hear the screw behind him radioing in what had happened.

They knew how dangerous Sullivan was, and knew they'd need more force than the screws had.

Which was why the firearms officers were deployed.

Normally it would take ten to twenty minutes for the firearms unit to assemble. Luckily for them, the firearms unit were training ten minutes away, and were able to arrive quicker than Sullivan had anticipated.

CHAPTER THIRTY-SIX

Sullivan ran across the top floor of E Wing. Inmates poked their heads out of their cells to see what the commotion was, and a few spice addicts begged for Sullivan to let them out too.

Sullivan ignored them. He took the steps two at a time until he reached the bottom floor, and sprinted to the wing's exit.

Another screw came running at him. He really did not want to hurt him. These screws weren't the criminals — they were people doing jobs. Some of them may even be honest.

But he had no choice.

He halted beside this screw and, before giving the man any chance to react, Sullivan placed a foot behind the screw's ankles and palmed his face, forcing him onto his back.

The man would not be badly hurt — just stunned long enough for Sullivan to find the right key. He left the wing and locked the door behind him to ensure no other inmates could escape as well.

He ran down a corridor, then around the corner and into another corridor.

He passed the chaplaincy. A few men were praying. He recognised some, and knew they were not religious — they just wanted an excuse to leave their cells.

Past this was the segregation unit, which was full of moans and screams. Sullivan passed them and reached the door, which brought him out between E Wing and D Wing.

The buildings looked even worse on the outside than they did on the inside. The bricks were crumbling, the paint was peeling, and the doors were cracked.

He ran past a cabin, and past the fence that surrounded the courtyard he had spent an hour a day in for the past few weeks.

He turned the corner, sprinting past C Wing and B Wing.

A screw saw him as he approached A wing, but Sullivan ran too quickly for him to comprehend what he'd just seen.

Sullivan heard footsteps behind him, and talking into a radio.

He had to keep going.

He turned another corner, and passed another fenced off courtyard, until he finally reached the main entrance.

A few heavy doors were either side of him, with signs saying *no smoking* and *CCTV in operation* — but the heaviest doors of all were the two large metal slabs in the way of him getting out.

He ran into the security office to his right.

Three faces turned to look at him. One at a computer, one looking at CCTV, and the other eating a curry.

They all stood and approached him, but he acted quickly. He charged toward the screw eating curry, snatched the knife from his hand and lifted him from his seat by the hair. Sullivan held his head back in one hand, and held the knife beside his throat with the other.

The others stopped approaching.

A few more screws who had been in pursuit burst into the room, and also came to a halt.

"Now, now, let's be—" said one screw, holding his arms out in a calming manner — but Sullivan did not care what he had to say.

"Let me out," Sullivan demanded.

"Let's not be—"

"I said let me out, or I will cut his throat."

Sullivan considered for a moment what he would do if these people did not comply. He did not wish to kill an innocent person.

But there were more lives at stake.

Luckily, he didn't have to deal with this possibility, as the man attempting to calm Sullivan said, "Fine, let's open the doors."

The door opened and Sullivan backed through, keeping his hostage between himself and the others.

He emerged outside, turned around, and stopped.

Three police cars were waiting for him, each with firearms officers using their car doors as cover. They pointed their guns at Sullivan, fingers itching over their triggers.

Sullivan wondered how he was going to get out of this one.

"Let the hostage go," they instructed.

A sudden headache took hold of him. His brain felt as if it was expanding. It was a sudden pang of alcohol withdrawal; he recognised the pain — he did all he could to ignore it. But it was clouding his mind. It was getting too tough to ignore.

"Let the hostage go," the voice repeated.

He couldn't do that.

If he did that, then—

The headache struck him harder and he fell to the floor. It took him a moment to realise he'd been tasered.

He tried to get up, but he was tasered again.

His headache grew worse. The last thing he saw before he passed out was the hostage running away, and the firearms approaching.

CHAPTER THIRTY-SEVEN

"Dad?"

Sullivan turned his head to the side. Opened his eyes a fraction. Squinted at the brightness of the sun. Covered his eyes. Turned his head away.

"Dad."

That voice.

He knew that voice.

It was a voice that brought him equal amounts of happiness and pain. It represented all that spurred him on to live, yet all that prompted his sorrow.

He opened his eyes slightly, and kept his eyelids apart just a tad until he adjusted to the sun.

"Dad!"

He sat up. He was on grass. Some kind of field or park or something.

She was standing above him.

"You're not real," he said, and even though he knew he was right, even though she wasn't really there, even though this was just another dream — he didn't care.

It seemed the only times he ever had a heart to heart with

his daughter nowadays was when she was manifested by his subconscious.

Something leapt upon his back.

He turned around.

It was a small dog. Jumping on him. Smiling, if dogs could do such a thing. Reaching its tongue out to kiss him, enthusiastic at the sight of him.

"I got a puppy," Talia said.

Sullivan had no idea whether she actually had a puppy or not. Hell, she may have twenty for all he knew. But his subconscious seemed to think she should have one, so she did.

Sullivan gave the dog a fuss then pushed himself to his feet.

Talia looked remarkably well. Those childish features she had in his memories were still there — the same nose, the same eyes, the same body shape. But now it was womanly. That nose was a woman's nose, those eyes had the pain of experience, and that body stood with the pride of battle.

And she smiled at him.

That smile was not hers. It was her mother's. She'd stolen it.

"So what is this?" he asked. "What do you want this time?"

"Don't be mad, Dad."

"Mad?"

"You're always so angry when you see me. So pent up."

"Trust me, it's not because of you."

"No. It's because of the weight of the world you put on your shoulders."

"It's put on me, I don't put it on—"

"You chose to do this mission. You asked Kelly if you could help. You agreed to go into the prison."

"If I don't, thousands of people will die."

She smiled. "Those people are not your responsibility."

Sullivan huffed and turned away. He put his hands in his pockets.

"If I can do something, then it's my responsibility," he said.

"Says who?"

"Do you know how many people I killed, Talia? Do you know how many people would still be alive if it weren't for me?"

"It wasn't your fault."

"I killed them."

"Because you were brainwashed, for Christ sake. At least you broke out of it. None of the others have."

"I'm a grown up, Talia. We tend to take responsibility for our actions."

"And you think saving these people will make up for it?"

Sullivan paused. Considered this. Bit his lip. Dropped his head.

"No," he said. "But it's a start."

"Dad—"

"If I'd have stopped the attack on Camden Market and Brighton Pier, I'd have saved more people than I've killed. What other situation would allow me to save that many people at once?"

"They weren't your fault."

"You don't understand."

"You did all you could."

"And it wasn't good enough."

"You—"

"Goddammit, Talia, what is the point of this? Why are you here? Why is my pathetic brain creating this conversation?"

"Perhaps it's the only way you'd ever listen."

He said nothing. She stepped closer, until she was right

next to him, and she took hold of his hand.

"Those people you're trying to save are the people who avoid looking at you when you stumble drunk down the street. They are the ones who won't sit next to you at the bar. They are the ones who condemn you to prison for committing all those hits, without understanding why you did them."

"I did them, Talia, it is my—"

"Responsibility, yes, I get it. But when does the responsibility for everyone else's lives end?"

He stared at her. So wise. So wonderful.

He wondered if this was actually what she was like.

"When does the suffering stop, Dad? When does *your* suffering stop?"

"When I've made up for it."

"And when is that?"

He shrugged. "Never, probably."

"Why torture yourself?"

He chuckled. "You have so much of your mother in you, do you know that?"

She let go of his hand. Took a few steps back.

"Where are you going?" he asked.

"Our conversation's over. It's time for me to leave."

"But, Talia—"

"You've got a terrorist attack to stop, haven't you? That's more important than me."

"Nothing is more important than you."

"That's nice of you to say, Dad. That really is nice of you to say."

He stretched his arm out for her, but she faded from view.

As did the grass. The trees. The blue sky.

His eyes opened to a grey ceiling, an empty cell, and narrow walls.

As his senses returned, he realised — he was in solitary confinement.

CHAPTER THIRTY-EIGHT

THERE WAS NO TELEVISION. NO SINK. NOT EVEN A window.

The air felt dirty and breathing felt strenuous. There was a toilet that was in no way concealed, a small bed with a hardened plastic mattress, and an artificial lamp hanging from the ceiling that changed the dark cream walls from a sickly colour to an even sicklier colour.

He had no paper. No pens. No books. Nothing to occupy his mind with. He imagined a great many people had gone crazy in this cell, and a great many people would go crazy again.

Luckily, this wasn't the first time he'd been in a cramped, dirty cell. He had suffered far worse conditions, and he had resisted madness before. Back when he was learning to become a Falcon, Alexander had created a training program designed to teach trainees how to endure being a prisoner, and it was an experience Sullivan would never forget.

"Very rarely does one of our assassins get caught," Alexander had said, pacing up and down the line of trainees. "In fact, only twice do I know of such a situation, and each assassin was dismissed upon their return for incompetency — not for being caught, but for the madness they returned with. And so, for the next month, you will experience what a prisoner of war may experience. You will either develop the mental strength to persevere, or you will prove to us that you are an unworthy candidate."

Alexander looked across the faces.

"Not all of you will come out the other side. You will not see me throughout this month, nor will you see anyone of the other trainees. Any pleas for help or for the program to end will be ignored. We will not stop, and your captors will not behave with sympathy. You will be getting the full experience. Is that understood?"

"Yes, sir," the trainees spoke as one.

"I ask now, as I will not ask it again, is there anyone who wishes to forego this program? Bearing in mind that, should you do so, you will be immediately discharged."

Alexander looked back and forth. No one raised their hand.

He nodded, turned, and left the room.

The trainees remained in line. In silence. Waiting for it to begin.

After a while, they began to look at each other, wondering what was happening and whether anyone was coming for them at all.

Eventually, they broke formation and discussed what a croc of shit this program was.

Sullivan did not join in.

He understood this was part of it.

Just as everyone began to relax and talk casually, the doors opened and armed men in military uniform and balaclavas burst in, shouting.

Sullivan was taken to the ground and a hood was placed

over his face. He stayed still and limp, allowing what was happening to happen.

He was dragged, his knees scraping against gravel, then placed into a cell. They removed his hood and closed the door behind them.

The cell was tiny; too small for him to be able to lie down. No bed. No window. No light.

Pitch black.

He wasn't quite sure how long he was left in there. He grew hungry and thirsty, and then grew hungrier and thirstier still — until it hurt. Until his stomach was so starved that it twisted in pain.

After what seemed like days, but was probably hours, the cell door opened and he was brought to his feet.

The light came on and he couldn't balance. He was dragged through to a small room with walls of stone and moisture in the air. They attached his cuffed hands to a rope and hoisted his arms up until he was dangling on the tips of his toes.

They left him like this. Unable to sit. Unable to properly stand.

Eventually, despite the constant discomfort, his body forced him to fall asleep.

Just as he found himself doing so, two speakers either side of his head burst to life. Loud, thrashing heavy metal music played in a burst of a few seconds, stopping him from drifting off.

He woke up. Looked around.

Darkness.

After a few minutes, he started to drift off again.

Just as he did, the noise burst through the speakers as it had before.

This kept going all night.

Someone came in with food. He was starving. His stomach was in agony, desperate for nourishment.

This person had mushed up beans or baby food or something. Sullivan didn't care. They took a spoon, scooped it up, held it out to his lips.

He opened his mouth and reached for it — but, just as he did, they took the food away.

They did this over and over.

Sullivan knew they wanted him to beg.

But he also knew that, if they wanted to keep him alive, they would need to give him food. So he was sure he'd have it eventually.

Once they had finished taunting him, they threw the food onto the grubby floor. They loosened the rope, allowing him to eat the food off the floor with his mouth. He had to fight with a rat for the last few bits, but he managed.

The next day he was waterboarded. Strapped down with his legs elevated in the air, his head covered with a towel, and water repeatedly poured on his face.

The next day he was left in a cell, naked, in the coldest of temperatures. Every now and then someone would come in and throw a bucket of cold water over him.

They electrocuted him, beat him, kept him in coffins, rubbed dirt into infected wounds, and forced him to endure rectal feeding and rehydration as an alternative to giving him food and drink.

This was repeated over and over.

When the month was up, Alexander entered the cell to collect Sullivan, expecting to find a shell of a man. Sullivan had heard the screams and begging of the other trainees from other cells. They had kept him awake throughout those nights where he had actually been allowed to sleep.

Alexander released Sullivan's restraints and shoved some clothes on the floor.

Sullivan dressed himself and stood up.

"Are you okay?" Alexander asked.

Sullivan grinned. "You need to tell your men they are a bunch of pansies."

Alexander smiled.

"Come on," he said. "Let's get back to work."

As Sullivan lay in solitary confinement of HMP Brenthall, he thought back to the cocky attitude he'd shown to Alexander, and how silly it had been to put on such a fake bravado. He'd just wanted Alexander to be proud of him. Truth was, he didn't sleep properly for a long time after that. More than three quarters of the other trainees did not show up to the next day's training. And those that did were changed. There was no more showing off — there was an understanding that this was serious.

Just like him, they did not want Alexander to see the nights where they woke up screaming, or lashed out in their sleep. Sullivan craved his approval and did not want to appear broken. He was a cocky nineteen-year-old who had already experienced a childhood of abuse.

This was just more abuse on top of it.

What the experience did do, however, was act as motivation. With the memory of what he'd been put through, Sullivan ensured that he was never, ever caught.

So this solitary confinement was nothing. If these screws thought they could break him, they evidently did not know who they were dealing with. He ignored the discomfort and focused on the mission.

He had to get out.

He had to get back to his cell.

He could not let Azeer give the go ahead for the next attack without Sullivan knowing when and where it would be.

So he stood at the small window in the door and stared into the empty corridor outside.

Shouts and screams of other prisoners provided the soundtrack for his impatience.

Eventually, footsteps approached. A screw emerged, talking with somebody that Sullivan recognised.

Jason Patricks. The prison governor. He'd only met him two weeks ago, but it felt like much longer.

"Governor!" Sullivan called out. This was his opportunity; Patricks had the power. If he spoke to him, then maybe he'd be able to get out.

But Patricks ignored him, just as he ignored the screams that came from the other cells too.

"Governor! Gov! Listen to me!"

Sullivan hated being ignored. It had always triggered him. But losing his shit with Patricks was not going to get his attention.

"Gov! Come on, please!"

Patricks almost reached the exit, engrossed in conversation with the screw.

Sullivan couldn't let him get away. He couldn't. But he had no way of getting his attention.

Then he recalled the picture in Patricks' office.

"I know Henry Jameson!"

Patricks stopped walking.

"I know him! I work with him! Please!"

Patricks left the screw at the exit and walked over to Sullivan's cell.

"How did you know Henry Jameson?" Patricks asked, and Sullivan could detect the sadness in his voice. If they were good friends, then Patricks would still be reeling from his death — enough that it sparked curiosity.

Sullivan hushed his voice so the screw couldn't hear.

"I work with him at MI5."

Patricks scoffed.

"I am," Sullivan insisted. "I swear."

"How do you know he worked for MI5?"

"Listen to me very carefully — there is going to be another attack. Azeer Nadeem is running the attacks from his prison cell. Jameson put me in prison, in that particular cell, so I can spy on him and find out when the next attack is."

"Well then you evidently failed. The attack happened, and Jameson is dead."

Hearing it aloud caused Sullivan to stutter, but he ignored it. He had to persist — he had Patricks listening; this was his chance.

"Jameson was at Brighton Pier because I spied on Azeer and found out this attack was going to be in Brighton. But there's another one, I swear, and if I am not there to find out when it is then no one will stop it."

Patricks leant toward Sullivan.

"Do you think I'm an idiot?" he said.

"No, come on, you have to listen to me—"

"I don't have to do anything. You are a serial murderer who just tried to escape prison. You are where you belong."

"Hundreds of people will die if you don't listen to me."

"Honestly, Mr Sullivan, this is the most ridiculous attempt at escaping punishment I have ever heard."

He turned and walked toward the screw waiting at the exit.

"No, come on!" Sullivan kept shouting. "You have to listen to me! You have to!"

Patricks and the screw walked through the exit and left without looking back.

CHAPTER THIRTY-NINE

A BUCKET OF FREEZING COLD WATER WAS ENOUGH TO WAKE Kelly.

Her memory replayed the last image it had. She was in a cell. Her hands chained to the walls. Stripped. Barely awake.

She was damn well awake now.

Except, she wasn't in a cell anymore. This room was made of stones. It had no natural light. She was shivering from the cold of the room, and the freezing temperature of the water. Her hands weren't fixed to the wall by chains, but handcuffed behind the chair she sat on.

To her right was a man wearing a poor attempt at military uniform. It was a camouflage vest over a black top. He wore a taqiyah — a skullcap worn by Muslims.

The man sitting opposite her wore a better-quality military uniform. He had a large beard and wore glasses. She recognised him. He was a general in the Alhami. His name was Imran Hashir.

She said nothing. She would not dignify them with conversation. They would get nothing but her silence.

"Agent Kelly Strong," Imran said. "Part of MI5. You are trying to figure out what our next target is, yes?"

Kelly wondered how he knew who she was, then remembered they'd had a leak at MI5. He probably knew everything about her.

"You did well, but our man was not going to stray from his duty. I hope you realise that Brighton Pier is now just rubble on a beach."

She instantly recalled what had happened. There was an explosion and a lot of people would be dead, including Jameson.

She had fallen into the sea, she remembered that... but what then? She fell unconscious... Why hadn't she drowned?

These people must have saved her. They wanted her alive, and there could only be one reason why:

They needed information.

Kelly had to resist giving it to them.

"I have one question for you," Imran said. "Should you answer it promptly, and to our satisfaction, this will all be over. Do you understand?"

Kelly did not respond.

Imran didn't need her to.

"How did you know about our demonstration on Brighton Pier?"

Ah, of course, his informant at MI5 would not know how Kelly had discovered there was going to be an attack on Brighton Pier. Imran would be thinking about Alhami's final attack; he would want to ensure that they wouldn't be compromised again.

She was their only way of finding answers, and that made her life far more valuable to them than it was to her.

"How did you know about Brighton Pier?" he repeated.

Kelly gave no reaction whatsoever.

Imran nodded to the soldier at Kelly's right. This soldier

picked up another bucket of freezing cold water and threw it over Kelly.

It was so cold that it was practically ice. In fact, she was sure she could feel a few bits of ice prick her skin. It hurt. She shivered profusely, her entire body tensing. Her feet and hands went numb.

Despite the pain, the true terror came in the humiliation of being sat there, naked, wet, and at the mercy of the man who represented Alhami.

"How did you know about Brighton Pier?"

She couldn't say anything. She couldn't let herself.

Whatever they did, she could not let herself.

Assuming Jameson was dead, there was no one else but Sullivan who knew how to stop the next attack. He may be stuck in prison with no one able to release him, but he was still their only hope, and she could not give him away.

She could not let the man she loved get hurt because of a mission she had brought him into.

For Sullivan's life, she had to persevere.

She took a big, deep breath.

She knew what happened to the prisoners Alhami took. She'd seen the remains. Barely any of them came out alive, and those that did were no longer able to function as a healthy person would.

A little bit of water would be nothing compared to what was to come.

It took everything she had to conjure the mental resilience she needed. It was time to take a deep breath, prepare for the worst, and endure.

"How did you know about Brighton Pier?" Imran repeated.

She looked into his eyes and gave him nothing.

Imran nodded at the soldier.

The soldier left for a moment, then came back in with

some kind of device. Kelly saw it and knew instantly that she was to be electrocuted.

The soldier put his boot on her back and pushed her to the floor.

Her face hit the hard stone and sent a vibration through her skull.

She felt the end of a wire attach to her genitalia.

"How did you know about Brighton Pier?"

Kelly closed her eyes and thought of home. Thought of her country. Thought of Sullivan.

Imran nodded at the soldier.

CHAPTER FORTY

Patricks continued his walk around the prison, as he did every week. He didn't want to be an invisible prison governor, like he knew many of his peers at other prisons were. He wanted to make his face known. He wanted to ensure that the prisoners knew who he was. Therefore, when it came time to discipline or to lend an understanding ear, he wasn't an unknown in their lives.

The one thing most of these men never had was consistency. Whether in their upbringing, their lifestyle, or what have you — and he believed that a prison was there to both punish and reform; even if the government had not given prisons the funding or resources to be able to achieve such goals.

Ralph, the prison officer accompanying him, took him through D Wing. It was the hour of the day that prisoners were let out, and he nodded at a few as he walked past their games of pools and conversations. Some hated him, of course, seeing him as the authority figure who, just like every other authority figure in their lives, was there to boss them around and take away privileges, and those prisoners scowled in an attempt to intimidate him. But there were also those who appreciated his presence; he had witnessed many inmates self-harming or attempting suicide or secretly crying over the inability to overcome their drug addiction, and those prisoners were the ones who would come to his aid should any of the more sinister inmates attempt to hurt him.

They left D Wing, and the prison officer accompanied him to the final wing. E Wing.

The atmosphere on E Wing was different. People played pool, but they did so silently. People watched television but sat stoically. In fact, there were very few inmates using the time outside in the courtyard that they were allowed.

He walked into the courtyard and saw why. Azeer Nadeem sat with his group, making a lot of noise. Rowdy banter, shouting out vile rap lyrics, and scowling at anyone who looked their way.

One prisoner stood up with a huff and went to leave. Azeer charged over to him, saying, "What are you huffing about?"

Patricks walked further into the courtyard and let his presence be known.

"Good afternoon, Azeer," he said.

Azeer let the prisoner walk on and turned to Patricks. Azeer said nothing, but he grinned; a knowing grin, like there was so much that Patricks didn't know.

"Is everything okay?" Patricks asked.

Azeer didn't answer. He looked over his shoulder at his crew, who all sniggered.

"I asked you a question, Azeer."

Azeer stepped forward. "I heard you."

Patricks glanced at the prison officer beside him, then back to Azeer.

"Is there a problem, my friend?"

"I don't know. Is there, gweilo?"

Patricks frowned. He resented the word gweilo. He did not use derogatory remarks about Azeer's race, and he did not expect Azeer to make them about his.

Before this confrontation could continue, the prison officer intervened.

"Alright, get back before I move you back to your cell," the prison officer said, and Azeer backed away, returning to his group whilst leering at Patricks.

There was something that bothered Patricks about this exchange — it was more than just an attempt at intimidation. He did not feel like the word gweilo had been used as a whim, but as a deeper hatred.

Patricks realised something and, as he did, he could not believe what he was about to do.

"Take me back to solitary confinement," he said.

"You want to go back to segregation?" the prison officer replied, as if this was the most preposterous thing anyone had ever said.

"Just do it."

The prison officer did not protest any further. He led Patricks through the prison, unlocking each door to let them through, then ensuring each of these doors were locked behind them.

They reached the door to the solitary confinement cells and, as the prison officer unlocked and opened the door, Patricks turned to him and said, "Wait here."

The prison officer waited as Patricks walked in and stopped at Sullivan's cell.

"Mr Sullivan," he said, pausing at the window.

Sullivan leapt up from the bed.

"Yeah?" he said eagerly.

Patricks hesitated.

This was a foolish move, yet his gut overruled any sense he had.

"If you are lying to me..." Patricks warned.

"I am not," Sullivan said, confidently. Patricks had imagined that most inmates in Sullivan's position would try to plead with him, but Sullivan didn't seem the man to beg — he was assertive with his desperation.

"If I find out you are, you will be spending the rest of your time here in solitary confinement."

"I'm not. Now get me out."

"Fine. I will get the officer to return you to your cell."

He looked Sullivan up and down, then turned to speak to the officer.

"There is one more thing," said Sullivan.

Patricks turned his head slowly, in disbelief at the impudence.

"Whatever could that be?"

"I am going to need an Arabic to English dictionary," Sullivan said. "And I am going to need it now."

CHAMAN, PAKISTAN

THREE YEARS AGO

CHAPTER FORTY-ONE

The training was relentless, and Zain was quickly learning to survive on little sleep. He spent most of his days wiping sweat out of his eyes and willing himself to persevere despite the stitches and fatigue.

Whilst he finally had a place where he felt like he belonged, he had still never felt so alone. He missed his parents. He hated to admit it, and he would never say it aloud, but he really did. He missed just being able to talk to them.

Unfortunately, rules in the compound were strict. He was not allowed a phone, meaning he couldn't talk to his family. He thought about sending them a letter, but he was rarely allowed away from the camp. He considered whether his parents ever wondered where he was, and if they would be proud of him if they knew what he was doing.

He tried to speak to the others, but conversations were always in Arabic, and those that did speak English often had a limited grasp on the language. He wasn't even allowed to know the general's names.

Azeer seemed to appreciate how isolated Zain felt and,

although he never acknowledged Zain's loneliness, he compensated for what Zain was missing in a friend and a father. He would often visit Zain to check how he was, and would tell Zain that he was eventually going to do something great with his life — and that his moment of glory wasn't far away.

Just a few years, in fact.

Meanwhile, he engaged in the training and committed himself as best as he could. After becoming annoyed with being unable to understand what was said during the talks, he took it upon himself to learn Arabic. Within weeks, he had a mild understanding of the language, being able to say basic words such as "hi," "how are you" and "what is for tea?"

He was taught how to make bombs out of ordinary household supplies. It didn't take long until Zain could take a fertiliser or paint stripper and create an explosive. Some others managed it quicker than he did, but it didn't matter, he still managed to build sufficient bombs within months.

He was taught how to assemble and shoot guns. AK-47s seemed to be the weapon of choice. It was a 7.62x39mm assault rifle originally developed by the Soviet Union. Zain didn't really understand what that meant, but that was okay. He just had to put the gun together and shoot.

At first, it took him a while, but he kept practicing it. He'd put the small end of the bolt into the bolt carrier. Rotate the locking lug. Slide it forward. Look at the guy next to him as he reached for the gas piston so he could see what it looked like. Put the gas piston in the end of the bolt carrier. Ensure the rear notches align. Insert the buffer. Align the notched end again. Put the dust cover into the notched area below the rear sight. Lock into place.

At first, this took him ten minutes; far longer than anyone else took.

Then it took him five minutes. Then two. Then one.

It didn't take long until he overtook everyone else and was able to assemble the rifle in under twenty seconds.

Then the rigorous, physically draining parts of weapons training began. He would have to crawl along the ground with his gun, leap over bags of sand, belly crawl through small holes in the ground, jump over tyres that had been set alight, crawl under barbed wire, learn how to attack in convoys and practise targeting his firearm.

He was told to memorise parts of the Quran. He was told to memorise parts of the Hadith. The Five Pillars. Sharia Law.

His Arabic improved and he could recite these in either language.

He prayed. He ate. He slept. Then he woke up the next day and it all started again.

He always looked forward to mornings the most. The drills and operational training took place during the day — the morning would begin with prayers, then a sermon.

It was the sermons that really excited him. They kept him motivated. They reminded him why he was enduring that day's gruelling training. Various generals spoke of championing the global Islamic community, of how fighting as an ally of Allah will grant them passage to Heaven, and how they would not be deterred just because they were the underdogs — someday the Islamic nations would become the most powerful nations, and they would end the West's humiliation of the global Islamic community. They were taught about martyrdom, saving the oppressed, honour, the victory of Allah, and the end of days — and the generals were always able to provide the right verse from the Quran to show that Allah believed in their cause, always reminding them that "Allah loves the doers of good." Even the Quran had managed to predict that "they will continue to fight you until they turn you back from your religion if they are able" — something they would never do.

Zain quickly became a martyrdom seeker. To give his life to fight the oppression of his brothers and sisters would be the most honourable death, and a sure path to Heaven.

They were shown videos. The kinds of images that showed the atrocities committed by the West in its mission to suppress the growth of Islam.

Such as the initial bombing of Iraq. The United Kingdom and United States searched for Saddam Hussain with bombs, and did not care who they killed. They watched footage of homes being lit up, and none of them had Saddam in there.

Videos of CIA training for enhanced interrogation techniques. Interrogators torturing their prisoners with waterboarding, sleep deprivation, controlled fear, and any other act they planned to use to get Muslims to talk.

A film of a bomb going off in a village in Afghanistan. British soldiers celebrated a job well done while mothers searched the rubble for their children.

All reminders of the many reasons they fought Islamic oppression.

Sometimes he thought, if those bastards who killed Fahad could see him now, what would they say? Would they fight, or would they run?

He could aim his AK-47 and spray them with bullets until they were nothing but a pile of bodies.

One day, after training and afternoon prayers, Azeer came to find Zain. He led him away for a private conversation.

Zain felt nervous, like this wasn't just an ordinary conversation. Like there was something Azeer had to say.

He was right.

"I'm moving you onto a different program," Azeer told him.

"What? Why? Have I not been doing well?"

"You are doing better than most, and that is why I am moving you."

"What program are you moving me to?"

Azeer smiled and put a hand on the young man's shoulders.

"The martyrdom program."

In that moment, everything fell into place.

Finally, he was going to get his chance to avenge the West's oppression on Islam.

He was going to be involved in a pivotal moment in this war.

And Allah was going to welcome him to Heaven with open arms.

HMP BRENTHALL, UNITED KINGDOM

NOW

CHAPTER FORTY-TWO

Sullivan had one recorder with a limited hard drive, so he had to work hard to ensure he translated everything quickly. He would record Azeer's conversations every night then, during the day, he would plug headphones in and turn the volume up as high as it would go. He would strain to hear the words but, covering his ears to remove all other noise, he would be able to make out most of them. It was a difficult language, but he'd spent enough time in the Middle East that he could at least tell the difference between the various words.

He hit pause at the end of every sentence. Wrote it down. Played the next sentence. Hit pause. Wrote it down. Played, pause, wrote. Played, pause, wrote.

He wouldn't have breakfast. He didn't have time. This would take him all morning, and well into the afternoon.

Then his cell would be opened, and they would be allowed into the courtyard. He would listen to Azeer and his gang leave their cells to intimidate whoever they chose to intimidate that day. He would watch as all the other prisoners went past.

And he would not join them.

Al would usually stop at his door.

"Are you coming out?" he'd say, followed by something like, "we still have a game of Rummy to play."

"Not right now. Maybe another time."

Al would look down, disappointed, and hobble away with his walking stick.

Once Sullivan had finished writing down all that was said, he was only halfway there. He'd transcribed the conversations — now for the translations.

He would use the Arabic to English dictionary to look up every word.

But he would find nothing. Just vague sentences, nothing conclusive. The attack was coming soon, but his intel gave him nothing to go on. Just ambiguous comments such as:

Kul shay jahez.
Everything is ready.

Kul shakhs ya'eref ma 'alyh fe'aloh.
Everyone understands what they are doing.

Qareeban.
Soon.

Still, he persisted.

Missing breakfast.

Turning down Al's requests for a game of cards.

Watching as Azeer left his cell, full of laughs and cajoling his mates.

Transcribing, translating, and repeating.

Until it came to four days before the thirty were up, time was running out, and he did not have a single thing to go on.

He stood, launched his pen across the room, and kicked the bed — an action that caused more harm to his foot than to the metal bed frame.

He hadn't even realised that their cells had been opened, meaning he didn't notice Al appear in the doorway behind him.

Sullivan stood, hands on hips, panting.

He recalled Sajid. His death. His pointless, meaningless death.

How many more Sajids were going to die?

Within days, maybe even sooner for all he knew, people were going to die, and the generic statements he kept translating were not helping him to figure out where or when.

"What on earth could be so bad?" came an ageing voice from behind Sullivan.

Sullivan turned, saw Al, and forced a smile.

"You're not used to being in prison, are you?" Al asked.

"Nah."

"You're in for murder. That right?"

"Yep."

Sullivan hoped his one syllable answers would tell Al that this wasn't the best time, and he was not in the mood.

It did not. Instead, Al hobbled into the cell and perched on the end of the bed.

Sullivan quickly shifted his pad and paper out of the way so Al couldn't see them.

"Oh, don't worry. I don't plan to read your memoirs, or whatever it is you're writing."

Sullivan said nothing. He wiped sweat from his forehead, despite how cold the cell was.

"Would you like to talk?" Al asked.

"I really wouldn't," Sullivan snapped.

"Do you know how long I've been here?"

Sullivan shrugged.

"Seventeen years," Al said. "Seventeen long years. And do you know how much longer I will be here?"

Sullivan didn't respond. He didn't care.

"Until the day I die," Al said anyway. "So you just learn to come to terms with it. Once you accept the way things are, it becomes a lot easier."

Sullivan scoffed. He'd spent too much time accepting the way things are. He'd accepted being a trained killer. He'd accepted being a wandering nomad. He'd accepted being a useless alcoholic.

Acceptance was what kept making him resolved to stay in shitty situations.

"You lost someone, didn't you?" Al said.

"What?"

"I saw your face when you watched the news of the terrorist attack in Brighton. Someone you know was killed, weren't they?"

Sullivan leant against the sink. Folded his arms. Dropped his head.

"Yeah," he admitted.

"A woman?"

"Yes."

"Was she a girlfriend of yours?"

What a question.

Was she a girlfriend?

She'd tried to be.

"Sure."

"That's the hardest part of this. Not being able to go to a funeral, or to say goodbye, or even know what's happening. You're trapped, and she's gone."

Sullivan nodded.

"Tell me about her."

Sullivan hesitated.

"Her name was Kelly," he said. "She was..."

"Beautiful?"

Sullivan chuckled. "You could say that."

"Yeah, they always are, the most dangerous ones. Always so beautiful."

"I think I was more dangerous than her."

Al nodded. "Didn't treat her right?"

"Could say that."

"Regret it?"

"I regret a lot of things."

"See, that's the thing about women. They will forgive far more than we ever would. They put up with our shit, and we resent them for it — how bad is that?"

Sullivan said nothing.

"But they are also intuitive — especially the beautiful ones. They know. Even if you don't say it, they know what you're feeling. So long as you kept fighting for her, she will have known how you felt."

"You think?"

"Oh, I know. She knew that you loved her, even if you didn't."

Al stood, using his walking stick to pull himself to his feet and regain his balance.

"Now stop moping around in your cell and come out and play a game of cards," Al said.

"Maybe later. I still have some things to do."

"Fine."

Al hobbled to the door.

"Hey, Al," said Sullivan.

Al paused and looked back. "Yeah?"

"Thanks."

Al nodded and left.

Sullivan returned to the translating, remembering why he was doing this.

Because Kelly would want him to.

Because he was the only one who knew.

Because he was the only one who could do anything about it.

So he kept going, over and over again, looking up each word. He found nothing, after nothing, after nothing.

His patience began to wane, and he grew more and more annoyed.

He just never found anything.

Until it was two days to go, and he did.

Unfortunately, it may already be too late.

CHAPTER FORTY-THREE

Kelly was eventually returned to her cell. She could not give them answers while she was dipping in and out of consciousness, and they needed her to recover before they delivered the next round of torment. They fixed her wrists to the chains that hung from the wall, leaving her to dangle with her knees a few inches above the floor.

She was beyond degraded and beyond hurt. She was broken. She was a wreck.

But she was also defiant.

She had kept her mouth shut and come to terms with the agony. Hopefully, they would not need her beyond their next attack; they only wanted to know how MI5 knew about the Brighton Pier bombing so they could ensure no one would stop the next bomb. The thirty days were nearly up, and after that, it wouldn't matter. Death couldn't be too far away. She just had to endure until then.

Or she could try to escape. If she was going to die anyway, what did she have to lose?

She had little energy left in her, but she had plenty of fight.

Her crotch was bloody and numb. Her body was empty yet heavy. Her mind was fatigued.

But her resolve was not yet dead.

All she needed was a chance. An opportunity. Her hands may be bound and her body may be hurt, but her awareness was intact. If she could just find her moment, an opportunity, some way she could fight back...

She shook her head. Was she being foolish? Delirious?

Most people in her position would accept their fate.

Actually, most in her position would talk.

She refused to be most people.

So she waited, helplessly dangling. She didn't know if they were watching her, it was too dark to know. So she played up to it.

She hit her feet around like she was finding it too painful. She thrashed out like she was desperate to lie down.

She closed her eyes and bowed her head, pretending she was just about to lose consciousness.

As soon as she did, more thrash-metal music played on loudspeakers next to her ears. It was a horrible, uncomfortable sound. Brief, yet painful. Her ears throbbed at the screams.

It ended, and she opened her eyes.

These were techniques the CIA had been known for in their fight against terrorism. They had called them Enhanced Interrogation Techniques.

The rest of the world had called it torture.

There was a whole list of things they could still try. She hadn't been waterboarded yet. She hadn't been subjected to any medically invasive procedures. Hell, she was surprised they hadn't molested her yet — surely that would be next?

She refused to accept it.

She refused to answer their questions, and she refused to relent in her determination to defy them.

She closed her eyes and played at being hurt. She was hurt, but she exaggerated it, made it more.

She did not want them to know she had her wits about her.

She did not want them to know that she had no intention of enduring anymore of these barbaric acts.

Just come and get me, she thought.

Then they'd see just how much this little, insignificant, inferior woman was capable of.

CHAPTER FORTY-FOUR

AZEER WAS HAPPY.

He couldn't have dreamt of a month as glorious as this, and he thanked Allah for watching over him in his mission.

He lay in bed, dreaming of the final demonstration. The oppressors of Islamic state, these infidels, these representatives of Satan — they would have no idea how much suffering they were yet to endure.

The biggest attack was coming.

Hasim turned his phone on, just as he did for two minutes every day, checking for messages from Alhami.

They never had any messages. Everyone knew not to contact unless it was an emergency. On this day, however, the phone vibrated and received a text.

Azeer asked Hasim, "Man haza?" *Who is this?*

Hasim hesitated.

"Enahu yureed attahadutha elayk." *He wants to talk to you.*

"Man?" *Who?*

They did not say the name of their confidants aloud, but Azeer had no doubt who it was. Hasim showed the screen to Azeer, and he was right.

He sighed.

Zain was a good man, and he was growing into a fierce warrior. But he was also young. Timid. Shy. Despite being such a brilliant servant of Allah and a soldier for the cause, he doubted himself too much.

"Aatini alhatef." *Give me the phone*.

Azeer snatched the phone and rang him.

Hasim looked out of the window, checking for any prison officers that may walk past.

He said, "Ma alamr?" *What is it?*

"Azeer, I just had to talk to you."

"Why?"

"I'm just..."

Azeer knew Zain wanted to say nervous, but did not have the guts to admit such a thing.

"Remind me what you're fighting for," Azeer said.

"I know what I'm fighting for, it's—"

"Then remind me."

Zain sighed. "Allah. My brothers. My sisters. For the slaughter of fallen Muslims."

"And who slaughtered them?"

Another sigh. "They did."

"Who is 'they'?"

"The Americans. The British. The French."

"Think bigger."

"The United Nations."

"You're right. That means no one is on our side but us."

"I just—"

"You just nothing."

"I'm worried I'll screw it up."

Azeer gripped the mattress.

"Remember your training. We have taught you all you need."

"I just—"

"I will be there with you."

There was a pause.

"You will?" Zain asked.

"Yes. I will be there to pray with you. I will be there to remind you of the glory you will find. I will be there to remind you of Allah's love."

"But how?"

"You leave that to me. It's not long now."

"Thank you, Azeer."

Azeer hung up and passed the phone to Hasim.

He turned and looked out of the cell window, over the empty courtyard below. Was it a mistake to have picked Zain?

No, of course it wasn't. Zain was trustworthy. He believed in the cause. He had trained harder than anyone.

He was the right person.

Azeer just needed to be there to give him a gentle nudge should he need it.

He looked at Hasim.

"Enna alwaqt qad han." *It is time*.

Hasim nodded.

Azeer's days in prison were up. He was ready to leave now.

During the thick of night, it was confirmed to him. He'd done a lot of pacing back and forth, a lot of worrying it may not happen, but it had.

Azeer's application for a prison transfer had come through.

One is never told when they are moving, but having a prison officer on his side helped Azeer. It meant he could be tipped off. That he could know in advance.

Before they went to sleep, and after they had finished praying, Azeer gave the final instructions to Hasim.

"Ta'akkad min anna aljame'a musta'edoun."

CHAPTER FORTY-FIVE

Patricks sat back in his office chair, trying not to break anything. He'd already broken his bin and knocked a mug off a shelf with the slamming of his door, but it wasn't enough.

He was a restrained man, yes. He was a calm, and authoritative — but, in one poor decision, that authority had been completely undermined.

How had he been so gullible?

Now even his staff, who were normally so intimidated in his presence, were mocking him.

"Heard you got conned!" one of them had said.

"It happens to all of us," said another.

"I mean, you know it was bullshit, right?" said a new prison officer, one who was too young and covered in pimples to stand up to even the least scary prisoners.

Even his wife somehow knew. As he arrived home, she was standing at the door ready to chuckle at his expense. That divorce was looming closer, and she would take anything she could do to get one up on him.

Sullivan had been so convincing.

He had played on Patricks' prejudices; perhaps even ones he wasn't aware he had. Azeer Nadeem was always so secretive, and had a group of Muslims who followed him wherever he went — but to say he was a terrorist...

Sullivan had conned Patricks, good and proper. He had made what the lesser educated members of staff would refer to as 'a mug' out of him.

Well, not again.

On his desk sat the final forms for Azeer's transferral to HMP Woodhill. Patricks added his signature to complete them.

Azeer would leave in the morning.

And Patricks would intentionally pass Sullivan's cell to mock him in return — to highlight that Sullivan would not fool him again.

Oh, what an idiot he was. Years of experience undermined in a moment. So much authority he'd had to earn, undone with the trick of one confident bastard.

He imagined what he could have said.

"Oh, you want to be put back in your prison cell? How would another week in solitary confinement work instead?"

He was tempted to move Sullivan straight back, but that would only make Patricks look weaker. As if he was trying to go back on his decision.

He just had to ride this one out.

You're a foolish man, he told himself.

He would not be taken for a fool again.

Not by anyone.

Not even Jay fucking Sullivan.

CHAPTER FORTY-SIX

Two days until the thirty were up.

The attack was imminent.

Time was running out.

Sullivan paced back and forth in his cell. It was taking him too long to translate. It was too time-consuming.

They wouldn't be talking about an attack that was weeks away, or even days. It could be a matter of hours.

And it was taking him longer than that to translate.

He tried going faster. He feared making mistakes, but he had no choice. Some words may end up being mistranslated, but he'd get the gist.

Until, finally, he translated a sentence that made his entire body tense.

"Etasil behem."

Phone them.

Phone who? Who were they phoning?

Sullivan listened to the next sentence.

"Ta'akad min 'ana hujum alghad jahiz."

He took it word by word.

Ensure.
That.
Everything.
Is.
Ready.
Sullivan stood.

Tomorrow's attack?

This recording had been done the previous night.

That meant they were talking about *today*.

"Shit," he said, rushed to the television, and turned it on.

On BBC One, they were showing a replay of *EastEnders*.

Countryfile was on BBC Two.

On ITV there was some daytime talk show where unattractive people argued about the trivial problems in their lives.

No breaking news. That meant the attack hadn't happened yet.

He kept translating. Kept going. He didn't know the target yet.

"Jama'atuna tantazir fi Heethro."

Our people are waiting at Heathrow.

Heathrow?

Did they mean the airport in London?

"My god," Sullivan muttered.

They had killed a lot of people at Brighton Pier, but that was nothing compared to this.

He grew dizzy and used the wall to balance himself, trying to stay calm. He was trained to stay calm.

Yet it wasn't so easy.

Heathrow Airport had thousands of people pass through it every day.

He rushed to his cell door. Where was the screw? Maybe they could alert someone?

Or maybe it would be tonight rather than this afternoon.

He hadn't translated it all yet, maybe Azeer had said something else about it.

He translated the next sentence.

"Sayanqulonani ela sijn akhar."

They will transfer me to another prison.

What?

Azeer was going to be transferred to another prison?

Prisoners were rarely told in advance and, if they were, they would only be told a few hours before. Yet Azeer had known.

The final sentence was spoken by the other voice. Hasim's.

Sullivan translated, praying to a god he did not believe in that there would be something he could use; a time, which part of Heathrow, something.

"Rijaluna musta'edoun lil'othour alyk."

Our men are ready to find you.

His men are ready to find him?

What the hell did that mean?

Then Sullivan realised; Azeer was going to be intercepted. The rest of Alhami knew he was being transferred.

They were going to ambush the van.

They were going to set Azeer free.

Sullivan could not let that happen. He could not allow Azeer to leave this wing; if he could stop that, maybe he could delay the attack.

He rushed to the window of his cell, trying to see to the one next to his. He couldn't see that far — but he did see a screw leading a man to the cell.

A man that was carrying a welcome pack just like he had a few weeks ago.

There was an absent bed in this cell, and someone was coming to replace it.

Which could only mean one thing — Azeer had already left.

CHAPTER FORTY-SEVEN

AZEER SAT IN THE BACK OF THE VAN, CONTENT AND COCKY.

Two other inmates sat opposite him. One with a large beard and a twitch. The other was a young man, a little too middle class to fit in with most of the inmates.

There were no windows, and no way of Azeer knowing how close they were, but he knew it couldn't be long now. His men had followed the vans driving this route numerous times, and had said it would take about ten minutes for him to arrive at the target location — which was along a country road where few cars were driven.

The van went over a few bumps. This didn't feel like a motorway or an A road; they were almost there.

He closed his eyes. Leant his head back. Felt the van come to a stop.

"What the fuck?" said a voice from the cabin.

Azeer's smile morphed into a large, satisfied grin.

He could picture it just as they had planned it. A car parked across the road to block the way, and a car following behind to block the van from reversing.

"I'll radio it in," said another voice.

No you will not, thought Azeer.

A spray of gunshots battered the van and shook the other two inmates. They both sat up, alert.

Azeer continued to rest his head back and enjoy the moment. He recognised the sound of the AK-47s. He'd trained enough people in how to fire them, how to assemble them, and how to target them, that the sound of their bullets was as familiar as his own voice.

The driver and his buddy would be dead now.

Azeer heard talking. He recognised the voices as they approached. The doors to the van opened, and Azeer squinted at the light. It wasn't that bright, but he'd been in darkness for fifteen minutes, which made even the smallest amount of sunshine become overwhelming.

His eyes quickly adjusted, and he smiled at the faces of his soldiers.

One of them rushed in and unfastened his handcuffs. The other two prisoners stared wide-eyed at the gun over his general's back.

"Maza anhum?" his general asked. *What about them?*

Azeer looked at the prisoners. Terrified. Pathetic.

"Etruk'hum," he said. *Leave them.*

He wasn't in the business of killing two insignificant morsels unfortunate enough to be in the back of a van with him. He had a far grander plan of death to attend to. Still, that didn't mean he was going to go out of his way to save them.

He discarded his handcuffs and stepped out of the van. As he walked toward the cars, his generals lit a Molotov each.

The prisoners saw them and tried to run. One managed to get out of the van and across the field, but the other stumbled and went up in flames as Azeer's men lit up the van in a glorious explosion.

Azeer climbed into the car. His thaub awaited him. Finally, he could release himself from his prison clothes.

He placed the ankle-length garment on, and smoothed down the sleeves. He sat back and rested as they drove past fields he hadn't seen in years, though they disappeared once they entered London. After an hour they arrived, passing Brunel University, turning around the corner from Hillingdon Cemetery and stopping outside a flat.

One of his generals opened the door for him, allowing him to step out of the car. He strode into the house and looked around.

"Ayn howa?" Azeer asked. *Where is he?*

He searched the living room, where a group of men were doing the final checks on the vest.

He searched the kitchen, where a group of men were going through a map of Heathrow Airport.

He walked upstairs. Looked in the bathroom.

Nothing.

Then he peered into the bedroom, and that was where he found him. Sitting on the edge of the bed, his fingers fidgeting, the face of a nervous wreck.

But Azeer saw through that, and smiled at the brave man that lay beneath.

"My brother," said Azeer, holding his arms open for an embrace. "It is good to see you."

"Thank you," said Zain. "It is good to see you too."

CHAPTER FORTY-EIGHT

SULLIVAN PACED BACK AND FORTH IN HIS CELL, JUMPING from one panic to another.

He was trained to be calm, dammit. He had to get a grip of himself.

A few footsteps passed his cell, and he ran to the small window in his cell door.

"You have to let me out, there's going to be a terrorist attack!" he shouted.

The screw ignored him.

"Let me out for fuck's sake, let me out! I'm not making it up!"

Sullivan knew that this was the kind of nonsense that screws heard every day. Prisoners banging against their doors, shouting that they needed to be let out, claiming they don't belong here. He heard those shouts all the time — mostly at night. The screw would assume Sullivan was just another crazy man, or was off his head on spice.

All the other prisoners had cried wolf enough times that he wouldn't be listened to.

But he had to try.

He had to.

"Stop ignoring me, I'm being serious! You have to listen to me, you fucking idiot!"

He knew this wasn't the best way to get the screw to listen but, once again, his anger took over.

He ignored his banging headache, he ignored his racing heart, and he ignored the sickly feeling in his stomach. He didn't know if these were symptoms of anxiety or lack of booze. He had to fight through it, he had to get the screw to listen.

Damn, how he missed the days that he would just wander from one place to the next, not giving a shit about such things.

Despite his ego, and despite the humiliation, he had no choice but to plead.

"I'm sorry, I didn't mean to call you that, you just have to listen, just listen, come on!"

The screw walked to the stairs. Looked over his shoulder. Grinned at another crazy inmate.

"I'm not crazy! People are going to die; you have to get me out of here!"

The screw chuckled to himself and walked down the steps.

"Fuck you!" Sullivan shouted, rattling the door, banging against it. "Fuck you and your judgemental looks you fucking *prick!*"

He tried to open the door. It would be useless, and he knew it, but he tried anyway.

He pulled it. Pushed it. Even tried using the end of his toothbrush to jimmy the lock.

He tried throwing his fist at the small window, but not even a bullet could penetrate it.

He stood still and realised he was panting.

He turned on the television. The news was on, but there were no reports about Heathrow yet.

But this hardly gave him hope. The light of early evening was descending, and there were only so many hours left for the attack to happen. He was running out of time.

He leant against the wall by his elbows, covering his head with his hands.

How did things get so fucked up?

His chest hurt. He took a few pills.

He stayed like this for a while.

He wanted to do something, but there truly was nothing he could do.

It felt so wrong to just be standing there, helpless, but the screw couldn't hear him even if they cared. The other prisoners had started shouting and would cover any noise Sullivan might make.

He had no one who could help him.

No one that would care.

What if he spoke to the governor? Patricks listened before, maybe he would listen again?

But how was he supposed to get the governor here? He could hardly give him a ring, could he?

He had to come to terms with it — he was completely alone, and unable to make any difference to what was about to happen.

He watched the news, hoping he was wrong. That he'd mistranslated.

It was all he could do. Just sit and hope.

He could have made a mistake, couldn't he?

Surely?

He'd made many before.

Except, he knew it wasn't a mistake. He knew he'd translated correctly.

But for now, at least, he could pretend.

CHAPTER FORTY-NINE

Patricks liked to walk around the prison after lockup. It was a time of day where he could truly gain a sense of the minds of these inmates.

He walked past the cells, listening to the shouts. Inmates openly made plans to deal spice to one another at a volume that everyone could hear. They shouted abuse and intimidation at those that they didn't like. They ranted about the prison officer on duty, declaring all the things they would like to do to them.

Even though the prison governor was walking through, they still subtly dealt drugs and bullied one another. He reminded himself that this wasn't because he was poor at his job, but was simply because of the state of prisons in this country. The UK was facing a prison crisis, and there did not seem to be a way out of this crisis any time soon. Half of these inmates would reoffend upon release. It was his job to prevent that, but there was little he could do in the current climate.

"Governor!" came a voice from a cell nearby. "Governor, over here! Over here!"

He ignored it. He wasn't prepared to be taunted or bullied like his prison officers were.

"Governor, it's me! Over here, it's me!"

It's me?

Intrigued, Patricks turned to look at who was calling him.

At the cell window was the face of Jay Sullivan. Patricks grew instantly furious.

"Governor, please, I need your help."

"What?" Patricks barked. "What could you possibly want?"

"Azeer Nadeem has been transferred."

"Yes, I am quite aware of what occurs in my prison, thank you."

"He knows he's being transferred; his group is planning an ambush."

Patricks scoffed and turned away.

"He is part of Alhami," Sullivan insisted. "He is the leader! They are planning an attack today!"

Patricks shook his head and turned back to Sullivan.

"Do you know how pathetic this is?" he said.

"What? No!"

"That you insist on involving me in this lie — you have already made a fool of me once; you think I'm going to listen to you again?"

"He is going to bomb Heathrow Airport — either you let me out so you can stop it, or you call the police."

"How could you possibly know what he is going to do?"

"Because I've been listening to their conversations, I've been translating."

"And you can translate as fast as you can listen, can you?"

"No, I have a Dictaphone and I've been playing it back."

Patricks felt his face redden.

"You have a Dictaphone?" he growled. "A banned item?"

Sullivan huffed. "That doesn't matter!"

"It bloody well does. My officers will do a search of your cell this evening, and we will see what other contraband you have, shall we?"

Sullivan sighed. Resigned. Any fight he had left drained out of him.

"You have to do something," Sullivan said. "You have to."

"I do not have to do anything. Goodbye."

Patricks walked away, leaving Sullivan shouting after him.

As he left the wing, Sullivan slumped down the wall and to the floor, his final opportunity gone.

There was nothing he could do but sit in his cell and wait to hear the news.

It seemed he would not be able to stop this attack either.

Once again, people were going to die because of his inability to use his skills for something useful.

Sorry, Kelly, he thought.

She would be so disappointed in him.

As would anyone else who had the misfortune of knowing him.

CHAPTER FIFTY

THE DOOR TO KELLY'S CELL OPENED, AND SHE KEPT HER head down. They dragged her through a corridor, and she kept her head down, pretending to be out of it.

As she was dragged, she caught a glimpse of where she was. It looked like some kind of basement, with two rooms — her cell and her torture chamber. She assumed she was still in the UK. She couldn't have been out of it for long enough for them to take her anywhere else — she'd have surely noticed if she was on a boat or a plane.

The open cuts on her knees stung as they dragged her through the room. The soldier placed her on the chair and went to put her handcuffs on, but Imran, sitting opposite her, waved his hands.

This was certainly a bit of good fortune for her. Retaliating would be far easier without handcuffs.

Then she realised, this meant that whatever he intended to do to her required more access to her body.

The soldier stood a few steps away. She scanned his body. He had a large hunter's knife by his ankle.

Imran sat back in his chair. He huffed. Folded his arms.

"How did you know about Brighton Pier?" he asked.

She did not react.

She just sat there, looking at the soldier.

Imran and the soldier exchanged a look of smug satisfaction.

They are hoping I don't answer...

Imran asked again, "How did you know about Brighton Pier?"

She glared at him.

He strode toward her so quickly that her eyes hadn't adjusted by the time his hands were on her throat. He swept her through the air and landed her on her back.

He removed his belt and wrapped it around her throat.

He squeezed. She couldn't breathe. He mounted her, lowering his face to hers. She could smell last night's meal on his breath.

She choked, hard. He kept her asphyxiated for longer than she expected, and it hurt.

Eventually, he loosened it slightly, just enough for her to gasp in breath.

"How did you know about Brighton Pier?"

She didn't answer.

He undid his trousers.

She mumbled something.

"What?" he said.

She mumbled something again.

"I can't hear you."

He moved his head closer. She mumbled once more.

"I can't hear you!"

He moved his ear beside her mouth.

"What?" he barked.

She didn't waste a moment.

She clamped her teeth around his ear and bit with all her might. He tried to throw her off, but she held on. She wrapped her arms around his neck and her legs around his torso, clutching onto him, feeling the thickness of his blood trickle down her chin.

The soldier approached. Before he could do anything, she'd reached her arm out, taken the hunter's knife from his ankle, and dug it into his leg.

She retracted the knife, lunged it into Imran's throat, and pulled it out as she let Imran go, leaving him to squirm

She looked at the soldier. He went to grab her, but she sidestepped and dug the knife into his throat.

Then she stood there. Watching the two men bleed, suffocate, and choke at her feet until they were still. It was a horrific sight, but the five years in the marines had hardened her.

Once they had stopped wriggling, she inspected their clothes. She had a bit of time — no one had come to interrupt them during the previous day's torture, and she expected no one to come and interrupt them today; they were alone, wherever they were.

She removed the soldier's clothes from his body and put them on herself. Collapsed. Leant against the wall. Felt the fatigue of her body pass through her. She released the tension in her muscles, and began to realise just how much pain she was in.

She stayed there for a while, panting. She didn't have the energy to escape yet, and she was enjoying the comfort of wearing clothes, as silly as that may seem.

Eventually, she stood, taking the knife with her, and limped to the door. She opened it slightly, peering out.

The cell she had been kept in was to her left, and there were stairs leading to a door to her right. She ran up them, as much as she was able, and paused.

She pressed slowly down on the door handle, and opened the door marginally, peering out.

It was a large hallway. Expensive ornaments on the wall next to paintings. A marble floor.

She crouched, moved into the hallway, and shut the basement door behind her. She stayed low, crept through the room. The front door was to her left, and another door was straight ahead, slightly ajar. Knowing she should just leave but unable to abandon her sense of duty, she peered through the crack in the door to the adjacent room.

Just as she did, she saw a man who struck terror through her entire body.

Azeer Nadeem.

How the hell did he get out of prison?

He wasn't alone. He stood with a few others. They were all praying.

In the corner, on a chair, it sat.

The bomb vest.

This was it. This was their preparation. They were about to commit the attack.

She looked around. Tried to think of what to do. She could hardly fight them. Not all of them.

The best thing she could do was follow them.

A Mercedes-Benz waited outside the window behind her, unoccupied.

She snuck out of the front door unnoticed and rushed to the car.

She opened the boot. Climbed in. Covered herself with a blanket and prayed they did not plan to use this part of the car.

She had no idea how she could stop the attack. The past few days were weighing heavily on her mind, and her body, and she found herself shaking. She could still feel the bolts of electricity gripping her muscles, could still feel Imran Hashir bleeding between her teeth, and did not know how long she could last in these cramped conditions — but it was the last piece of torture she would have to endure.

I killed a man, her mind kept telling her: *I killed a man, I killed a man, I killed a man.*

But she blocked it out. The trauma could wait. There would be plenty of counsellors waiting for her at MI5.

All she had to do now was be patient, and hope that she could figure out what to do.

CHAPTER FIFTY-ONE

Zain stood in a row with his brothers, Azeer to his left.

They faced toward Makkah, and spoke together, "Allaha Akbar. Allaha Akbar."

Zain placed his right hand over his left, then placed them both on his navel, in unison with the others.

"Bismillah ar-Rahman ar-Raheem," they spoke.

Zain tried to keep his mind focused on what they were doing. To keep his mind focused on his god. On his task.

On the honour bestowed upon him.

"Al hamdu lillahi rabbil 'alameen."

He did not think about his family. Refused to think about his father. Refused to picture the look on his face, or remember the eyes of disappointment from the last time he saw them.

He told himself not to recall how his father had said he was a disgrace, and that this was not true Islam.

He reminded himself that his father was wrong.

He had to be wrong.

"Ar-Rahman ar-Raheem Maaliki yaumid Deen."

He remembered that he trusted in Azeer.

Azeer had guided him on the right path. He had guided him on Allah's path. He had guided him to this point in his life now, and he was ready.

He was ready.

He was.

Really.

They finished the Surah Al Fatiha and began the Ruku.

Zain kept his appearance in a state of concentration, just as he was taught. No fidgeting. No looking around. Keeping his focus on his god.

He bowed with the rest.

"Subhanna rabbiy-al-'adheem."

He will be in Heaven soon.

"Subhanna rabbiy-al-'adheem."

Father doesn't matter.

"Subhanna rabbiy-al-'adheem."

He trusted in Allah. He trusted in Azeer.

They stood.

"Sami'allaahu li man hamidah."

He refused to recall the look on his mother's face. The way she had cursed the day she'd given him life. The words she'd said as she cried.

"Rabbanaa wa lakal-hamd."

He'd never seen her cry like that.

But she hadn't witnessed Fahad die.

He had.

And he knew he was doing the right thing.

He did.

He knew.

He really knew.

Zain followed the others in lowering himself to his knees and placing his toes, knees, hand and forehead upon the ground.

"Subhaana rabbiyal-a'laa."

He knelt up, and returned to the floor. Knelt up, and returned to the floor.

"Rabbighdfir lee, warhamnee, wahdinee, warzuqnee, wajburnee wa rasooluh."

He had a younger sister. She would be a woman now, but he remembered her as a child. She dated an infidel behind her parent's back.

She would not find Allah's mercy.

He knelt and turned his head to the right.

"Assalaamu 'alaykum wa rahmatullaah."

Azeer knew best.

Zain had trained for this.

He'd trained.

He'd been selected.

Specifically.

Him.

Chosen.

It was an important mission.

He had to do it.

He had to.

For Allah.

For Azeer.

For the Islamic state; in the name of the oppression put upon them for so many years.

He turned to his left.

"Assalaamu 'alaykum wa rahmatullaah."

They finished.

They stood.

They remained silent as they each said their own silent prayers.

Zain bowed his head, trying to make it look like he was doing the same.

Trying not to think about what he was about to do.

He had to be strong.

He was strong.

Stronger than anyone.

He would show them.

They finished and Azeer walked up to Zain. With an encouraging smile, he placed a hand on Zain's shoulder.

"It's time," Azeer said.

Zain nodded.

"Get the car," Azeer told one of his generals.

Azeer was right. It was time.

They climbed into the car and placed their guns by their feet — out of sight of prying eyes, but easy to access when they needed them.

It would take them ten minutes to drive to the airport, then it was up to him.

He would be in paradise soon.

CHAMAN, PAKISTAN

TWO YEARS AGO

CHAPTER FIFTY-TWO

ZAIN HADN'T LEFT THE COMPOUND IN YEARS.

At first, it had been strange. Now it felt liberating. In the UK he would always be checking over his shoulder, ensuring he had his knife on him, looking back at the face of everyone who stared at him, worried that either he would be killed, or he would have to kill them.

Despite being isolated in this camp, he felt safer than he ever had.

And he did not feel like an outsider. He did not feel like someone people avoided eye contact with because they feared what he was going to do — here, he was with his people. He had learnt enough Arabic so he could talk to them, and although they did not talk about anything personal, such as where they came from or who their families were, they still achieved an element of comradery. They would discuss that day's speech, or encourage one another in particularly gruelling days of training.

Even when he was younger, and he hung around with Fahad and his friends, he never really felt part of the group. They mainly hung around together for strength in numbers

— it was safer to be with others like him. But he had separated himself from them when they all had come to terms with Fahad's death so easily. Like it was normal. Like it was okay. Like it was just part of life in Britain.

They accepted it and moved on, had families of their own, and only thought of Fahad when it came to the anniversary of his murder, or in the moment of silence that followed when Zain brought his name up. To them, it was an uncomfortable memory they did not want to think about.

What infuriated Zain most about these so-called friends, what really incensed him — was that they had stopped being angry.

Zain had never stopped being angry.

The moment that his fury ended was the moment that Fahad died in vain.

The moment he simply accepted that it had happened and allowed himself to let it go, or move on, was the moment that Fahad's memory died, and his death became nothing.

Zain would never stop fighting those who had hurt his brother.

Never.

And, although he was with Allah now, Zain often wondered who Fahad would be should he still be alive. His father wanted him to be a doctor. He was considering law. He was smart, and he could have done either.

Now he was just a tombstone that people forgot to visit.

"Zain," Azeer said, prompting Zain to end his endless thoughts. His dinner was in front of him, and he hadn't touched any of it.

"Yeah?"

"Come. Let's talk."

Zain left the rest of his food and followed Azeer out of the tent. They walked around the edge of the compound, and

Azeer did not talk straight away. This was fine. Zain was used to Azeer considering his words.

Eventually, after a few minutes of strolling, Azeer spoke.

"I've been watching," he said. "You have done very well."

"Thank you, brother."

"I mean it. You have taken to the martyrdom program better than anyone else."

"I appreciate it. I've been trying."

"You have. You definitely have. Now it is time for you to go home."

Zain stopped walking.

"I am home," he said.

Azeer smiled. He was always so calm, always so wise. There was never a moment he saw Azeer lose control. He always knew what was best.

"That you are," Azeer said. "But I mean your other home. Where you came from. The United Kingdom. England."

"Am I not doing well enough here? Am I not trying hard enough? Please, just tell me what I've done, and I'll—"

"Oh, Zain, you have it all wrong. You are not going back there to live. You are going back there to die."

"I don't understand."

Azeer put his hand on Zain's shoulder and led him to a large rock, where they both sat.

"We are planning three strikes against our enemies — three demonstrations that they will not suppress the growth of the Islamic state any longer."

"When?"

"Two years from now. We are planning them all to occur within a matter of weeks, for maximum effect."

"And you want me to help?"

Once again, Azeer smiled at Zain's naivete.

"I want you to be the main event," Azeer said.

"I don't understand."

"You are receiving a great honour, Zain. You will be our final martyr, and you will find your place with Allah."

Zain was astounded. He couldn't believe it.

"Thank you," he said.

He was finally going to play his part in this war.

Yet, his main thought was not on his action to come — but on the prospect of seeing his family.

He missed them terribly, and he was excited to see them again.

He just hoped they would be as eager to see him.

HMP BRENTHALL, UNITED KINGDOM

NOW

CHAPTER FIFTY-THREE

A YOUNGER SULLIVAN STEPPED OUT OF THE CAR AND walked with his arms folded to the cemetery's edge.

Alexander went to enter, noticed his prodigy standing still, and turned to him with hands on hips.

"What are you doing?" Alexander demanded.

"This is bullshit."

"Stop being an idiot and move."

Alexander went to walk into the cemetery, but Sullivan remained at the entrance.

"I won't ask again," he said.

Reluctantly, Sullivan walked forward, his arms folded, his head shaking.

"I still don't get why I have to do this," he said.

"That is why I am the one who is training you, and you are the one who is being trained."

"But I don't—"

"Tell me, oh wise one," Alexander said sarcastically, jabbing his finger at Sullivan. "Who recruited who?"

"I get it, you're in charge, it just doesn't—"

"You're damn right I am."

"But I don't see why—"

"Because of this. Everything you are doing right now. This petulant teenager act. This fuck-you attitude you have when it comes to something difficult."

"Something difficult? I let you torture me and I did not complain once!"

"You let us?"

"Fine, I couldn't do much about it — but I did it."

"And this is worse?"

"Yes."

"Because it makes you angry."

"It makes me furious."

Alexander stepped toward him. "Then that is why you have to do it."

Alexander marched on.

Sullivan huffed, and followed.

After a few minutes, Alexander had led him down a path, past several rows of small graves. Some of them cared for, some of them not.

Then he paused by one particular row, forcing Sullivan to stop with him.

"It's the sixth and seventh one in," Alexander said.

Sullivan went to look, but he couldn't.

He could see them. He could even see a bit of the name.

But he couldn't walk toward it.

Even in death, he couldn't dignify this man with his attention.

He turned away, covering his face.

He refused to let himself cry in front of Alexander. Alexander was training him to be a killer, not a weakling. He could not let him see this.

Alexander said, slowly and calmly, "Let it out."

"What?" Sullivan said, wiping his eyes, still fighting them back.

"I said let it out."

"But an assassin doesn't—"

"I will tell you what an assassin does and doesn't do."

"But I can't let him win like this."

"Jay, you are young, and you are foolish, so I will spell it out for you the best way I can — you are no good to us angry. You are no good to us emotional. You are no good to us a wreck."

Sullivan covered his face.

"But you don't overcome all of these feelings by burying them deep down. I need you to face them, so you can be rid of them."

"I can't—"

"You can, and you will. I can't let you out in the field if I don't trust you to be calm — and you can't fight someone else while you are still fighting yourself. So drop your hands, let yourself cry, and go look at the damn grave."

Sullivan dropped his hands, as he was told. His eyes were red and damp, but he did not let them leak any tears. Instead, he did as he was instructed, walking slowly along the graves, until he reached the sixth and seventh ones in.

They were buried together. Even after what his father had done to his mother, they were buried together.

"I hate you," Sullivan muttered, staring at the name of the sixth grave in:

Kevin William Sullivan.

"I hate you so much," Sullivan continued.

His fists clenched.

He looked at the seventh grave:

. . .

Michaela Sullivan.

"I hate you too," he said. "I hate you for staying with him. For allowing it. For never—"

He stopped talking.

He was too angry.

He thought he was upset, but he was angry.

"I can't," he told Alexander. "I can't. I can't stop being mad at him. I can't forgive him."

Alexander sighed. "Well then there is an alternative."

"What?"

Alexander walked along the graves until he reached Sullivan's side, and looked over his shoulder.

"Use it," he said quietly.

"What?"

"Use the anger. If you can't fight it, harness it. Let it power you. Let it fuel you. Let it be your strength. See your father's eyes in the eyes of every man you kill. Believe it to be him."

Sullivan nodded.

He could do that.

In that way, he could have his revenge. He could kill his father a hundred times over. He could show him what was right and what was wrong.

Yes, that's right.

He'd show his dad.

He'd show him what he deserved.

With a large, sudden roar, Sullivan swung his fist at the small grave. His knuckles were left to bleed, but he shattered the stone across his father's name.

He swung his fist again.

That was when Sullivan woke up, plunging his fist into the wall of his prison cell.

He had no idea how he'd manage to sleep. Then again, he had barely slept at all in the last few days, so it was inevitable he'd fall asleep at some point.

The news was still on. It was still early evening. He'd only drifted off for ten minutes or so.

There was still no report on an attack.

He thought about what Alexander had said. To see his father's face in his enemies made him a ruthless opponent, but it had also turned him into an angry man. A bitter man. Whilst he had turned his back on his training, his anger was the one thing that remained.

Right now, he was furious. He had lost. Kelly was dead, yet he was alive — which was too much of an injustice — and he could find no way out of his cell.

He heard a few steps outside his cell.

A key in the lock of the door.

What was this?

"Step back!" demanded the screw.

Sullivan leapt up.

"What's going on?"

"Step back, contraband check!"

Sullivan was momentarily confused, then recalled what Patricks had told Sullivan after he found out Sullivan had a Dictaphone.

They were going to do a contraband check on his cell...

This was it. This was his opportunity.

He had to be cool. Wait for the right moment. Despite the little time he had, he had to be patient.

He walked to the far side of the cell and pressed himself up against the wall, as was routine for this type of inspection.

The door to his cell opened and three screws walked in wearing rubber gloves.

"Stay against the wall," one instructed him.

They were honest people doing an honest job, and he didn't want to cause lasting damage to them.

The only question, then, was how he would incapacitate all of them without killing them.

He did not want them to call the police like the last time he tried to escape.

As the one nearest to him lifted his mattress, he watched the back of their head, and readied himself for a fight.

CHAPTER FIFTY-FOUR

The nearest screw was a man. About six foot two. Heavy set.

The others sifting through his mattress were a middle-aged woman and a younger, more timid looking man.

They would be easier to pick off, so he decided to start with the bigger guy.

"Against the wall," the big guy said, noticing Sullivan eyeing him up.

Sullivan did as he was told.

"Turn around."

Sullivan did not.

"I said turn around."

Sullivan kept his face blank. His body still.

He needed Big Guy to approach. He needed to wind him up enough that he had no choice but to use force.

"You deaf?" Big Guy said. "I said turn around."

Sullivan remained as he was.

"Oi, stop ignoring me, I said—"

Big Guy approached, lifting his hand. Sullivan took that

hand, bent it backwards so as to snap it, then took hold of Big Guy's head and rammed his skull into the sink.

Big Guy slumped onto the floor in an unconscious mess.

The other two looked at Sullivan, terrified.

The woman reached for her radio.

He leapt forward, took her arm, threw her over his shoulder and onto the floor. He took the PAVA synthetic pepper spray from her belt and emptied enough into her face to keep her from getting in his way.

Timid Guy attempted to make his escape. Sullivan threw out a foot and swiped Timid Guy's legs out. The sound of his head hitting the floor echoed around the cell.

Timid Guy had handcuffs on his belt.

He took them, cuffed one of Timid Guy's wrists, pulled the handcuffs around the leg of the bed, and cuffed the other wrist.

He took the woman's handcuffs and did the same to her, then did the same to Big Guy. He removed their radios from their belts and stepped back.

Big Guy would have a headache when he woke up, and would need to go to the hospital for his wrist. The other two would feel pretty humiliated, but he had done no lasting damage.

He took a set of keys from one of the belts, then discarded the radios into the wing.

He retraced his steps from a few weeks ago, except this time, he would not make the same mistakes. He would not head straight to the gates. He could not risk the police being called again.

Instead, he diverted his route past the segregation unit and towards the governor's office. He'd been there when he'd first arrived, and although his memory was patchy, he could just about recall the route.

He tried to remain quick and agile, but there is a fine line between stealth and speed. He had to remain unnoticed by other screws and the cameras, but he also had to be quick. Still, this was what he had been trained to do, and he did it well. Once upon a time, he could make his way through a heavily guarded, well-monitored building completely unnoticed. His feet were heavier than they used to be, and he had a constant feeling of sickness that reminded him how little whiskey he'd had in the past few weeks, but he made it, staying close to the wall and checking the direction of the CCTV cameras.

Just before the governor's office was a small staff kitchen. He would need a weapon to coerce the governor into cooperating, so he went into the kitchen, only to find a screw toasting some crumpets.

The screw reached for his belt, and Sullivan didn't waste any time — he struck him over the head with the toaster and the screw collapsed, knocked out. Sullivan removed the screw's belt and threw it out of reach to ensure he was not able to radio in about the escaped convict when he eventually woke up.

Sullivan went through the draws, found a large kitchen knife, and turned to Jason Patricks' office.

"Here goes..."

He kicked the door open and charged in.

CHAPTER FIFTY-FIVE

"What on earth!" Patricks declared. "How dare you! Who do you think you are, coming in here and—"

Sullivan, feeling he needed to intimidate this guy before he threatened him, took hold of the side of his large, wooden, polished desk, and turned it upside down, throwing it across the room.

Without the desk in front of him, Patricks looked quite exposed, and couldn't help but quiver.

Sullivan took hold of Patricks' collar, lifted him from his seat, held him against the wall, and placed the tip of the knife against his throat.

"You know what I am, yeah?" he said, his voice low and husky.

"Yes, yes I do!"

"So you know how many people I've killed?"

"Yes!"

"You know what I am capable of?"

"Yes!"

"Good — then you know to do everything I say. You are going to lead me out of this prison, into the car park, and into your car. I am going to keep my knife hidden, but the second you signal to someone else that you are under duress, I will use it to cut your throat. Understand?"

"Yes, yes I do!"

"What am I going to do?"

"Cu— cu— cu—"

"Say it."

"You're going to cut my throat!"

"You believe me?"

"Yes!"

"You bloody well should. Now move."

Despite the man being relatively innocent, Sullivan still gained a little satisfaction from taking such a narcissist down a peg or two.

He followed behind Patricks as they left his office, and Patricks led him to the main gate.

"Sir?" one of two prison officers said, looking at Sullivan, confused.

"Open the gate."

"But, sir, we don't have any information of a prisoner being transferred, should we—"

"I have had the call myself. I am the governor, you will do what I say, now open the damn gate."

Good boy, thought Sullivan.

Patricks had evidently read his file. Sullivan's record was enough to incite the kind of fear that would make a man piss his pants and hand over his wife.

As it was, he just wanted Patricks' car.

They left the prison, and Patricks led Sullivan across the car park.

"Give me your car keys," Sullivan instructed.

Patricks reached into his pocket, pulled them out, and handed them over.

"Which one is it?"

"The Ferrari."

Of course it was the Ferrari. His prison was understaffed, underfunded, and under-resourced, but he still ensured he had a big enough pay-check to buy a nice, shiny car.

Still, at least it was a fast car.

"Get in the passenger seat."

"What? I thought you just wanted the car!"

"Do as I say."

Like it or not, he would need someone to phone the police as he drove.

They got in. Sullivan turned the ignition and sped away with a loud rev of the engine.

He put the radio on to check the news — still nothing.

Even so, Alhami would undoubtedly be there by now.

They were just waiting for the right moment, and Sullivan had no idea whether he would get there in time.

CHAPTER FIFTY-SIX

Zain sat in the back of the car, Azeer beside him.

But he didn't look at his trusted mentor.

Instead, he looked out of the window, with his hand rested on his fist, and butterflies charging around his belly.

They drove past Holiday Inn. Zain recalled a time when he was four, possibly five, arriving at this hotel, with his baby sister in the back of the car next to him. It was one of his earliest memories. His parents had bickered a bit and he was annoyed. It was a strange situation, as his parents never bickered — yet he had a very real memory that his mum was somehow mad at his dad.

Yet, as soon as they had arrived, his parents were full of smiles, and they walked into the hotel hand in hand.

Past a row of houses to his right was Heathrow Primary School. School had finished, but there were still students there, waiting to be picked up following after-school clubs. Quite a few of them carried instruments; violins and cellos in their cases, plus boxes that probably carried something like a flute or clarinet.

His friends had taken the mickey out of the school

orchestra and sniggered at what dorks they were. He hadn't. He'd always watched them with envy. He'd always wanted to learn to play an instrument.

They went through the tunnel to the Inner Ring, and passed a bus that had just begun to unload. A group of people, possibly eighteen to twenty, just beginning adulthood, walked off, wearing the same t-shirts; blue with *Build a School* in bright orange writing.

They pulled up outside the terminal.

The SatNav said, in its toneless, woman's voice, "You have arrived at your destination."

They were here.

It was time.

CHAPTER FIFTY-SEVEN

Sullivan raced down the fast lane of the M25.

Signs for London Heathrow Airport became more constant, and planes flew overhead.

They couldn't be far.

"Do you have a phone?" Sullivan demanded.

"Yes."

"Get it."

Patricks reached into the glove compartment and took out his phone. It was an iPhone — one of the newer ones.

"Phone 999," Sullivan said.

"And tell them what?"

"There is going to be a terrorist attack at Heathrow Airport."

"You actually believe—"

"Just do it!"

Sullivan did not have time to stay calm. Patricks was beginning to regain a little bit of confidence, and was becoming a little defiant, so Sullivan lifted the knife. He didn't directly threaten Patricks with it — he just kept it between his fingers, making sure it could be seen.

"Now," Sullivan demanded.

The phone shook in Patricks' hand. He dialled 999 and put the phone to his ear.

Sullivan drove down the slip road of junction 14 and onto Bath Road.

"Hello?" Patricks said. "Police please. Yes, I, er—"

Patricks looked at Sullivan. Sullivan looked back.

"Please help," Patricks said, suddenly speaking quickly, "I'm being held against my will, there is a man escaped from—"

"Goddammit!"

Sullivan snatched the phone away and put it to his ear.

"Hello? Yeah, there is going to be a terrorist attack at London Heathrow."

"Excuse me?" the operator said.

"You heard me — another attack by Alhami, Azeer Nadeem is running it, you need to get police there quickly."

"Okay, sir, what do you—"

"No questions, just do it."

Sullivan hung up and chucked the phone out of the window.

He glanced at Patricks.

"Arsehole."

Sullivan drove around a roundabout and onto Wright Way. He entered the tunnel and began his drive toward the terminal.

But it was at the end of the tunnel that he was forced to stop.

A queue blocked his entry.

He wasted no time. He opened the door and ran out, leaving Patricks in the car. He didn't have time to queue; he had to run.

He sprinted as fast as he could, ignoring his stitch. He

leapt over a bench. Dodged a bin. Ran as hard as his aching legs would let him.

He saw him. Azeer, in a car, in the drop off bay, with others, just outside the terminal.

Someone stepped out of the car. A young man. Looking nervous. Looking everywhere.

His chest looked slightly bigger than it should — like his muscles did not match his legs.

It was a bomb vest.

That was him.

He was the suicide bomber. And he was entering the airport.

LONDON HEATHROW AIRPORT, UNITED KINGDOM

CHAPTER FIFTY-EIGHT

Sullivan was too far away. No matter how fast he ran, he could do nothing to stop the bomber from entering the airport. The young man disappeared amongst the crowds, which would make him harder to find. Sullivan studied him quickly, ensuring he would recognise him — red top, with short, black hair, and converse trainers.

He kept running toward the entrance and, as he did, Azeer Nadeem stepped out of the car and locked eyes with him.

Azeer grinned.

"You," he said.

Sullivan ran across the road. A car screeched to a halt and Sullivan slid across the bonnet, ignoring the horn and the obscenities aimed in his direction.

"I knew you were not just an inmate," Azeer said.

Sullivan was closer. Fifteen yards now, if that.

"You can't stop it now," Azeer said.

Watch me.

But, true to Azeer's word, he was not planning to let Sullivan get any closer.

He took out his AK-47.

"Shit!"

Azeer did not care who was nearby. He did not care which civilians he would hit. He did not even care about being caught. Why would he? There were police at the airport, but they could do nothing against an AK-47; they would have to wait for the firearms unit to arrive, and by then the airport would be in flames.

Once again, it was up to Sullivan.

Azeer opened fire, forcing Sullivan to dive behind a parked BMW. He stayed behind the wheel, using it as his barricade.

I'm fucked, he thought. The bomber was in the airport, and he was stuck behind a car, listening to the thuds of bullets meant just for him. Soon, there would be little of the car left.

He reminded himself that he was trained for this; this was the kind of situation he was an expert in dealing with.

At the same time as thinking this, he couldn't help but admit that he was completely, totally, and utterly fucked.

CHAPTER FIFTY-NINE

Not long after the engine had died, the shooting had started.

Kelly stayed where she was, listening to the onslaught of bullets. It was loud and, with her head already pounding, she could do nothing but listen. The shooting was right next to the car, and if she were to get out, she would be shot. She had to be smart. Choose the right moment.

But how the hell would she know the right moment?

She could see nothing, and the pains of her body were making it difficult to think. Her body was no longer in agony, but it was still stinging. Her fingers and toes, which had been so numb, were starting to throb. Even worse, the mental battle was getting tougher.

She was struggling to think clearly.

But she knew she should wait. She'd stand no chance of stopping anything with a bullet lodged in her head.

Then again, what chance did she have anyway?

She had a knife. She could not get past the shooter with a knife. And even if she did, what could she do against the bomber?

This is so stupid.

What was she even thinking, getting into the boot? She should have gone straight to the police.

But what then? Tell them there was an attack coming, but she had no idea where it would be?

No, she had to wait.

Rue her bad decisions and wait.

The bullets continued, and she wondered if they were ever actually going to end.

CHAPTER SIXTY

"Assalamu alykum."

Peace be upon you.

Azeer's final words repeated over and over again in Zain's mind.

The sign above indicated that terminal two was to the left and terminal three, four and five were to the right.

The vest felt heavy. His legs felt heavy. His mind felt heavy.

Two young women passed him, pushing a trolley of luggage, and he watched them as they entered the lift.

"Did you want to come in?" they asked him, holding the doors for him.

He shook his head.

The doors closed and they left.

He heard bullets from behind him. Outside, Azeer was firing his AK-47.

The police must have arrived before they expected.

He considered the hundreds who were about to perish.

He reminded himself why they must perish.

He took a deep breath.

He had to move. Azeer trusted him.

He found his legs slowly carrying him deeper into the airport, walking stiffly and robotically.

His eyes widened, and he saw the life of every face he passed in slow motion.

They didn't look at him — they were too busy with their mobile phones, or children, or luggage, or checking tickets, or looking at the screen for their terminal, or pretending he didn't exist, and he wondered why no one looked at him if they were all so afraid, if everyone believed him to be a terrorist, if everyone here thought he was suspicious, then why was not a single person looking at him and asking *should I be scared?*

These people were evil. This country was evil. It had committed evil acts.

Its people had killed Fahad. Its people had repressed the Islamic state. Allah would not suffer an infidel to live, and neither should he.

But he didn't feel isolated or shunned or discriminated against. In this airport, when people were at their most tense, no one seemed to be wondering why this nervous looking Muslim was walking through the airport.

He closed his eyes.

For Fahad.

For Azeer.

For my fallen brothers and sisters.

He was panting and wheezing. He became aware of every part of his body. His fingertips tingled and his feet tensed, and his legs ached, and his brain was heavy, and his skull was tight, how could a skull be so tight, it felt like his brain was bursting against it — why was it expanding and expanding so much and why was no one suspicious?

It felt like everyone was looking at him, yet no one was looking at all.

He did not need to pass through security. He could just enter the space where all the shops and people were and rely on the strength of the blast.

It would make the biggest statement ever made on British land.

He would be a hero. A martyr. Allah would welcome him to paradise with open arms.

But all he could see was an old couple sat on a bench, holding hands, next to a younger couple with a laughing child and why, why, why did everything seem so big and so small at the same time?

"Stop this, Zain," he told himself.

This was no time for doubt. No time for second thoughts. No time for hesitation.

Azeer relied on him.

Allah relied on him.

He was one serving God and that was how it would be.

Fuck his family if they didn't understand.

Fuck these people who hated his religion.

Fuck everyone.

He hated them all.

No one ever cared. No one ever spoke to him like a man, like a person, not until he met Azeer, not until Azeer showed him the love that even his own family were unwilling to give.

Enough deliberating.

Enough thinking.

He reached into his pocket.

His fingers flexed around the detonator, and his thumb traced the outline of the trigger.

CHAPTER SIXTY-ONE

Azeer held his finger against the trigger and sprayed his bullets over anyone who dared look.

Jay Sullivan was behind the car. Concealed, but his cover was temporary. Soon there would be little left of the car.

Azeer couldn't stop grinning; he'd never believed that things would go so well. He'd been worried that he'd be caught, that Alhami would not manage to succeed. The paranoia this country had about terrorists means that they barely trusted a Muslim to walk down a street. Yet here he was, standing for his brothers and sisters.

His ammunition ran out.

He didn't need to rush to replace it. His brothers had left the car and begun firing also. He allowed himself a moment to watch and take satisfaction at what they were achieving.

He noticed an empty police car, and a few officers using it as cover. Even the law was cowering. Azeer assumed these were police that regularly patrolled the airport — they would not deploy ordinary officers to fight an armed assailant, they would only use their firearms unit. They were so backwards in this country — the everyday police officers don't carry guns, so by the time armed officers arrived, most of the destruction would already be done.

And what did the unarmed officers do who were already here? Hide behind their car! Do nothing to protect the civilians! These people knew nothing of sacrifice. Azeer would not hide from his enemy, whether they had a gun in their hand or not. He would stand and fight and die willingly should that be what Allah decided; not cower and allow more civilians to die.

All three of them had now directed their guns at the police car. Most civilians had either fled, or were lying in pools of blood across the road.

Azeer laughed.

"Allahu Akbar!" he shouted, ensuring that the glory of the moment went to Allah — it was Allah that had guided them here, and it was Allah that had given him the fortune of being able to create this moment.

As he revelled in the glory and gunfire, he did not notice the man running to his left, and the sound of heavy footsteps approaching.

CHAPTER SIXTY-TWO

Glancing back, Sullivan could see the terror on the police officer's faces. This was not something an officer normally experiences in their career. Not in the UK, anyway. He'd seen gunfights in the US. He'd seen gunfights in South Africa. He'd seen gunfights in Iraq, and he'd even been involved in one in Pakistan. But these officers were unprepared. He could see the fear on their faces, and he could see how torn they were — wanting to protect those caught in the crossfire, but also wanting to keep their lives.

This wasn't a chance for them to be a hero. They were attracting the attention of the gunfire, and that's what Sullivan needed them to do.

It allowed him to run across the car park, staying low, and to the concealment of another car.

From here, it was maybe a ten-yard dash to Azeer. He was sure he could make it. Only problem was that Azeer wasn't alone — there were two more of them.

He wondered how trained they were. Alhami would have had rigorous training in their camps, Sullivan was sure of it — but would they be too much for him?

Years ago he wouldn't even have hesitated — nothing was too much for him.

He needed to think like that again; with that indestructible confidence he used to have.

Of course he could do it.

He had to do it.

What else could he do?

He'd seen the boy enter the terminal. He would be in the heart of the airport by now. He would be getting ready.

Sullivan didn't have time for self-doubt.

He ran. Charged from behind the car. Sprinted toward Azeer.

He growled as he came close, roared, and Azeer turned to look at Sullivan just as he dove Azeer to the ground with a rugby tackle.

The other two turned their guns on him and hesitated, not wanting to accidentally shoot Azeer. Sullivan was quick — not as quick as he used to be, but not as sluggish as he felt — and was able to duck beneath one of the guns, then take hold of the second guy's gun and push it upwards, into the guy's nose.

He twisted the gun toward the first guy and shot him in the head, then twisted the gun back and shot the second guy through the underside of his chin.

He turned the gun to Azeer, who had taken to his feet with his own gun and pointed it at Sullivan.

They remained in this stand-off without talking.

Sullivan would have been content to stay like this, but he didn't have time; he had to get to the boy.

He stepped forward until their guns crossed paths, and each barrel was inches from the other's face.

Sullivan swiped his gun against Azeer's, and both AK-47s went sliding across the ground and out of reach. This was to Sullivan's advantage; he hated guns. Guns ran out of bullets —

but he never ran out of the resources he could use from his environment.

Before he could search for an item he could make into a weapon, he felt Azeer's fist land on his jaw.

Azeer packed a far heavier punch than Sullivan had expected, and it knocked him a little.

Sullivan went to retaliate, only to find another strike land in his face.

He felt dazed.

Azeer sent another fist in, but Sullivan finally rediscovered his instincts and blocked it. This still didn't mean he noticed the other fist coming in, pounding the side of his skull and knocking him to the floor.

Azeer mounted him and threw a few more punches.

How had Sullivan been so stupid?

This wasn't a situation he was used to. He could fight off ten armed men — yet this one man had forced upon him the indignity of being taken to the floor, and was now beating the shit out of him.

Sullivan blocked a strike, but Azeer simply took hold of that arm and moved it out of the way so he could strike his other into his jaw.

Sullivan tasted blood.

He was groggy.

He was losing.

CHAPTER SIXTY-THREE

Wasn't this guy supposed to be some big assassin or something?

Azeer had seen him on the news before his big arrival. People were talking about him. A former assassin for the British government. Someone Azeer had truly really wanted to kill; who knew how many of his brothers and sisters Sullivan might have killed over the years in the name of this country.

And now he had his chance. The fool was below him, barely able to fight back, and barely moving.

All Azeer had to do now was finish him off.

Sullivan tried to roll onto his side, and he couldn't even do that. His eyes were barely open, his breath was struggling, and his face was a bloody mess.

"Your country turned on you," Azeer said, "yet you still fight for them."

Sullivan looked for his gun.

"How pathetic," Azeer persisted.

The gun was across the floor, past a few more deserted cars.

But one of the guns of the men Sullivan had killed was within arm's reach, so Azeer picked that one up.

"If you were one of us, we'd be celebrating you as a hero. Instead, they see you as a nothing."

Sullivan tried to roll over again, but he was unable to.

He groaned, and Azeer felt a sting of pride. Not only had he set up this magnificent thirty days of justice — he had beaten the country's most lethal product.

The gun's magazine was empty. He released it.

Where were the other magazines?

They were in the car. The one Sullivan lay next to, moaning.

Azeer grinned and went to open the car door.

Sullivan said something.

"What?" he said, pausing.

Sullivan said something again, but it was mumbled.

"Spit the blood out," Azeer said. "It's making you talk shit."

Sullivan spat the blood out, and did so over the bottom of Azeer's thaub.

Azeer was incensed. He crouched next to the soon-to-be-dead infidel. A gun would be quicker than Sullivan deserved. Azeer discarded it and placed his hands around Sullivan's throat.

How dare he?

How fucking dare he?

Azeer pressed his thumbs against Sullivan's larynx and squeezed.

Sullivan choked.

CHAPTER SIXTY-FOUR

What Sullivan had in fact tried to say was, "You're an idiot — because it was true.

Sullivan had endured far more rigorous training than even Alhami could provide.

He had endured torture. He'd spent a month being a prisoner of war, learning to endure the worst torment his enemy could provide. He had been waterboarded, deprived of sleep, starved, beaten, electrocuted; every piece of torture Alexander could imagine Sullivan having to face, he had faced.

And he had learned how to overcome it.

This meant that a little beating was not going to deter him.

Bruises? Blood? A dip in and out of consciousness?

That was nothing.

So when Azeer leant down and placed his thumbs on Sullivan's neck, Sullivan did not react straight away.

He waited for a moment. He needn't be hasty. He could survive a little oxygen deprivation.

He released his mind of all urgency.

Flexed his arms.

And, in an abrupt movement bound to perplex his opponent, he thumped his fists against the inside of Azeer's elbows, forcing him to release Sullivan's throat.

In a swift move, he hoisted Azeer upwards, giving him a chance to roll Azeer onto his back.

Azeer tried to swing his fists again, but it did little to deter Sullivan. He took hold of Azeer's head, lifted it up, and smacked his forehead hard into the pavement.

This wasn't how he wanted to do it. This was the man who had killed Kelly, and hundreds of others. Sullivan wanted to see Azeer's face as he suffered.

He lifted Azeer up by the collar, held him high, then slammed him downwards so that his head pounded against the edge of the car bonnet.

He did this again, and again, and it was on the third time that Azeer lost consciousness.

Sullivan did not stop there.

He continued until he heard the crack of Azeer's neck, and again until he heard the crack of Azeer's skull.

He stood, wiping sweat from his forehead and splatters of blood from his hands.

Azeer's eyes were open, but they did not move. He bled, but he did not breathe.

He was finished.

Sullivan was exhausted. His body ached, his face throbbed from his beating, and the adrenaline that had allowed him to fight Azeer was quickly fading.

But he was not done. There was still an attack he had to stop.

He ran into the airport, looking back and forth.

He fell. His legs gave way, but he pushed himself back up, and limped on.

He had to find the boy.

He had no idea what he'd do when he found him, but he had to.

He could warn these people and urge them to leave but there would be no guarantee that they wouldn't be caught in the blast — and if people began to leave, it would spook the bomber and make him hit the detonator.

For now he just had to find the boy, and convince him not to press the detonator.

It was his only chance.

CHAPTER SIXTY-FIVE

Zain's thumb stroked the trigger.

Funny, how something so small could cause such devastation.

So much power in just the lightest of touches.

Azeer would be wondering why he hadn't pushed that trigger yet. Zain could not wait any longer.

He closed his eyes. Readied his thumb. Held his breath, and—

"Wait!"

He opened his eyes.

A voice amongst the mass of conversations stuck out.

It was a British voice, and not one he recognised, yet he felt like it was for him.

But it couldn't be. No one knew what he was doing. They did not know why he was there. The detonator was in his pocket, no one could see it.

"Wait, please don't!"

But there was the voice again, rising above all others.

Only a few people glanced in the direction of the shouting, then carried on with their lives. But Zain kept watching.

A man emerged from the crowds. He was older than Zain. He hobbled and limped. His face was a beaten mess. He looked bedraggled and wounded.

Yet, there he was, continuing to edge toward Zain.

"I know what you're doing," the man said.

He knew what he was doing?

How?

No, he couldn't. He had no idea. He was lying.

"Please, just — just listen."

"You don't know who I am," Zain said.

"Why don't you tell me?"

"Fuck you!"

"Look, I—"

"Fuck you, stay back!"

"Fine!"

The man paused, only steps away, and held his hands in the air.

A moment of silence lingered. People hurried past without paying them any attention.

"What's your name?" the man asked.

"Why does it matter?"

"Mine is Jay Sullivan. People normally call me Sullivan, but you can call me Jay if you like."

Why was he telling him this?

If this man knew what Zain was doing, he should be tackling him to the ground, forcing the detonator off him, trying to kill him.

Yet he was just stood there, talking.

"So if you call me Jay, what do I call you?"

"... Zain," he reluctantly answered.

"Zain. Great name. It means beauty and grace, doesn't it?"

Zain nodded. How did he know that?

"Funny. I would never refer to myself as graceful. Would you?"

Zain shook his head.

"I'm sure your parents had good reason for calling you that."

Zain grew angry. "Don't talk about my parents."

"Okay, fine, I won't."

"I know what you're trying to do."

"What am I trying to do, Zain?"

"You're trying to talk me down. To persuade me not to do this."

"You're right, Zain, that is what I'm doing. I'm trying to talk to you, trying to persuade you not to hit the detonator — but, mostly, I'm trying to figure out what could make a young man like you, with his whole life before him, be so angry?"

Zain felt his face curl up and contort. His fists clenched, his heart raced; who the fuck was this guy?

"You know nothing!" Zain said.

"Then tell me."

"I'm not telling you shit, you're not stopping me doing this!"

"Okay, fine, maybe I won't stop you. But you could at least tell me why you're so angry."

"I'm not—"

Zain stopped himself. He felt tears accumulate, and he fought them away.

He flexed his fingers around the detonator.

Enough talking.

He closed his eyes.

"Who was it?"

He opened them again. "What?"

"I said, who was it?"

"Who was what?"

"Obviously, there must have been a person who persuaded you to do this. And I don't just mean Azeer Nadeem — I mean someone else."

Zain refused to talk. But, somehow, his face gave it all away.

"You lost someone you cared about, didn't you?"

Zain shook his head.

No.

Stop it.

This was not happening.

"I watched someone I love die too, you know," Sullivan said. "I was only sixteen, but I watched it, and I don't think anyone could have stopped me from hating the world after that."

Zain shook his head harder. Fuck this guy. He wouldn't understand.

"That anger made it so much easier to kill the bad guys — and it was clear who the bad guys were, because my mentor told me who they were. Sound familiar?"

"I am not like you."

"Azeer used your loss to teach you that killing is necessary, didn't he?"

"It is necessary."

"Is it?"

"Go to hell, what do you know?"

"Actually, when it comes to killing out of anger, I probably know more than most."

"Shut up! You don't know a thing! You don't know what it's like to be angry all the time because you did nothing. You probably had parents who'd wipe your arse for you."

"The only thing my father wiped was my blood from his fist. I never had a family who gave a shit if I lived or died. In fact, it was my parents I saw die, after my father killed them both. But what about you, Zain?"

The man stepped closer.

Zain backed away.

"Do you have a family who care?" he asked.

"You don't know shit about my family."

Sullivan relaxed his body. He stopped edging closer.

"Then tell me," he said.

SOUTHEND, UNITED KINGDOM

ONE YEAR AGO

CHAPTER SIXTY-SIX

Three tentative knocks on the door. Shifting weight from one foot to the other. Sweat trickling down his forehead.

Zain could not remember ever being this nervous.

He hadn't called. He'd thought about it, but wasn't sure what they'd say. Instead, he decided to show up and hope for the best.

The door opened.

His mother's eyes flickered in recognition. There was a moment of hesitation, then she enveloped him in her arms. He said nothing, just held her, staying in the moment, until finally she pulled herself away and looked at him.

"Oh, Zain," she said, her eyes damp, and hugged him again.

Over her shoulder, and further into the house, he saw his father. Standing in the corridor. Watching.

His mother let him go and, guided by her hand on his back, Zain entered. He walked up to his father and paused.

"Hi," he said.

His father put his arms around Zain and gave him a stern hug.

"Come," he said. "Let's get you a drink."

Within five minutes they were sitting in the living room with cups of tea. Zain didn't particularly like tea, but his family weren't to know that. Maybe once they would have, but not now. So he took it and placed it next to his seat, leaving it untouched.

His mother spoke quickly, but his father stayed quiet.

"We have been so worried, we had no idea where you have been, what you've been doing. Have you been at college? University? Oh, it doesn't matter, you are back now. Are you back for good? I mean, I've left your room just as you left it, but..."

She trailed off, as if realising that she had not left space for answers to any of her questions.

"I am back," Zain said. "I'm staying with friends, but I'm back here for a while."

"How long is a while?" his mother asked, then quickly added, "oh, it doesn't matter. Just so long as you're okay."

"Where have you been?" his father asked.

A moment of uncomfortable silence descended, and his mother tried to fill it.

"Your sister is doing very well, Zaynab is at university now, she's studying law, she's found herself a man and is engaged, he's very nice, his name is—"

"I would like an answer to my question," his father interrupted.

This time, his mother stayed silent.

"Where have you been?" he repeated.

"Away," Zain said.

"Where?"

"I'm not allowed to tell you."

"You are my son. You will tell me where you have been."

Zain looked down. He wondered how much his father knew. He wondered whether he'd be disappointed.

Then again, why should he care? If his father was a true Islamist then he would be supportive, not dismissive.

"Pakistan," Zain finally answered.

"Pakistan!" his mother repeated. "How on earth did you — what were you doing there?"

Zain didn't answer.

"Oh, it's okay, you're back now and—"

"What were you doing there, Zain?" his father asked.

Zain paused. "Training."

"Training for what? I imagine it was not university."

"No."

"Then what?"

Zain looked around, considering how much to tell him.

"You're one of them, aren't you?" his father said.

"One of who?"

"I heard rumours. I heard people saying terrible things. But I said, not my son, wherever he is, he is strong, he is noble, he is brave, he would not be one of them. But you are. Aren't you?"

"One of *who*?"

"Don't take me for a fool."

"Do you mean the Alhami?"

"You know damn well that's what I mean."

"And what if I was? Wouldn't you be proud?"

His father dropped his head. Shook it.

He had never seen such disappointment on his father's face before.

Zain fought through it. He was doing the right thing, even if his father couldn't see that.

"You are to come home," his father said. "You are to stay here. You are to leave your friends—"

"No."

His father looked horrified.

"No?" he repeated.

Zain took in a deep breath. He could not back down, never mind however much it hurt.

"The Surah says, but if ye cannot, and of a surety ye cannot, then fear the fire whose fuel is men and stones — which is prepared for those who reject faith."

His father scoffed.

"Please," he said. "I had been studying the Quran for decades before you were born."

"Then evidently you didn't study it very well."

His father stood. His face turned red. "You cannot guide those you would like to, but God guides those He wills, He has best knowledge of the guided — what about that verse? Did you read that one?"

Zain went to respond, but his father did not let him.

"God does not forbid you from being good to those who have not fought you in religion or driven you from your homes — what about that one?"

"But they have driven us from our homes, they—"

"God does not love corruption. Surat al-Baqara, 205. And that one?"

"They are the ones who are corrupt."

"No, my son, it is you. You are the ones who are corrupt, for trying to poison my religion by picking out the pieces of the Quran that suit your will."

"It is Allah's will."

"Are you so sure?"

"And you are the one who is picking parts of the Quran to suit you. I have studied it, and I have—"

"You studied the parts the fools who taught it to you wanted you to study." Zain's father stood. "You are nothing more than a victim of their sickness. You are tainting our lives, and you are causing friction between us and everyone else in this country."

"They caused the friction when—"

"When they went into one of their many wars, I bet?" His father stepped closer, casting Zain in his shadow. "Let me ask you a question. Who do you think gave the go ahead for the war? The entirety of this country, or just the few who lead it?"

Zain shook his head.

"You sound like one of them," he said. "You abuse Allah."

His father shook his head.

"You are a fake Muslim," Zain continued. "You are a kafir."

His father's face changed. He went from forceful authority to shock. From resolve to shame.

Zain retreated in on himself. That was the most outspoken he'd ever been, it was the most aggressive he'd ever felt himself become, and it was at a family that he loved.

But there were more important things than his family.

His cause. That was more important. Azeer relied on him.

His father wasn't right. He couldn't be.

Could he?

"This is not what Fahad would have wanted," his father said. "There is a big difference between the people who hurt him, and the people you hate."

Zain did not respond.

This was as much confirmation of Zain's stubbornness as his father needed.

"Get out," said his father.

"Oh, please, let's just—" his mother attempted, but was ignored.

"Get out," his father repeated, his voice low and quiet. "Get out of my house, and never return."

Zain looked to his mother. She looked away.

Zain turned and left without looking back.

LONDON HEATHROW AIRPORT, UNITED KINGDOM

NOW

CHAPTER SIXTY-SEVEN

Despite all he believed, all he had fought against, and his struggle against Azeer — Sullivan did not see a terrorist in front of him.

He saw a boy on the verge of committing a terrible, atrocious act, yes — but he did not see a member of Alhami.

And he did not see a monster.

He saw a scared, desperate young man, who had witnessed awful things, and had suffered because of those awful things.

A troubled man, who was punishing himself as much as he was punishing everyone else.

A boy on the verge of choosing a life that would not only harness his anger, but would build on it.

Sullivan saw *himself*.

But Zain could still avoid Sullivan's fate, and Sullivan was desperate to help him.

He decided to take a different tact.

"I was brainwashed too, you know."

"What?" This seemed to make him angrier. "I have not been brainwashed! I have been set free!"

"So was I."

"Stop it! I am nothing like you!"

"The only difference is which side brainwashed us. For me, it was the British government. For you, it was Alhami. But they are both the same."

"They are not both—"

"They really get to you, don't they?"

Zain's face was a mess of emotions. Sullivan could see fear, he could see fury, but he could also see hope.

Then again, he could also see the detonator in Zain's pocket, and Zain's hand wrapped around it.

This was a fine line he was treading, and the wrong word either way could sentence the people around them to death.

So many people. Families, friends, lovers — there were hundreds who might die.

But Sullivan did not judge Zain for that. Yes, he was about to do a bad thing, but Sullivan had done plenty of bad things.

He'd killed families. He'd killed friends. He'd killed lovers.

He hadn't done them all at the same time, but he'd done them. It had taken him years to realise he had been manipulated, and he'd made a mistake.

Zain did not have years. He had minutes.

Seconds for Sullivan to save this world from another person like himself.

"This person you lost... They tell you all kinds of things to make it seem like his death had a purpose, don't they?"

Zain furiously shook his head. "You don't know—"

"They offer you something that makes you feel like their death wasn't in vain. That it could mean something. But Zain, guess what?"

He stepped forward and Zain did not step back.

"It's not worth it," Sullivan said. "It's never going to be okay."

Sullivan could reach out and grab that detonator. He could grab with his right hand, then choke Zain with his left.

But he didn't.

Instead, he looked the boy in the eyes. Zain shook his head, trying to be assertive in his defiance, but Sullivan could see it was wavering.

This was no longer about saving an airport full of innocent people — it was about saving a troubled, desperate boy.

"Was this person a family member? A friend? A brother?"

"They are all my brothers!"

"They are, I'm not saying they are not." He edged forward. "But nothing will make that death okay."

"You're an infidel. You deny the spread of Islam. You are not in Allah's—"

"But do you really believe that, Zain?"

Sullivan placed a hand on Zain's arm.

He heard heavy footsteps in the distance behind him. He glanced over his shoulder.

Firearms police had arrived. They were still far enough away that Sullivan and Zain remained unnoticed, but Sullivan knew they were looking for a young Muslim male like Zain. They would be ready to take down anyone they even suspected of trying to blow up the airport.

He didn't have long to save Zain's life.

The tannoy announcement began. "Ladies and gentlemen, this is an emergency. Please proceed to the nearest exit. I repeat, please evacuate the airport, as calmly as you can."

Sullivan ignored the people rushing past. He focused on Zain's eyes.

"Those firearms officers. You see them behind me?"

Zain looked over his shoulder and nodded.

"If they even suspect who you are and what you are planning to do, they will shoot you in the head. Do you understand?"

"But how do they know—"

"Because Azeer Nadeem shot civilians outside."

"Is Azeer okay?"

"No, Zain. He isn't. I killed him."

Zain scowled. He went to step away from Sullivan, but Sullivan took hold of his arm and kept him close.

"Now's not the time. You can take vengeance on me all you want later. But for now, you have to make a decision."

"What?"

"Either blow up this airport, or leave with me."

Zain stared at the firearms police, who were shouting for everyone to get down.

"And I'd hurry, Zain. Because it won't take them long to find you."

Sullivan smiled a sad smile.

This poor human being looked so, so scared.

"So what do you want, Zain?"

CHAPTER SIXTY-EIGHT

"So what do you want Zain?"

Those words rang around Zain's mind like they were echoing around a cave.

He stared at the firearms units.

Not long.

He had a detonator in his hand.

He had a man saying he could help him escape.

And yet the question, *what do you want,* was the one he could not escape.

What did he want?

He wanted Fahad to never have died. He wanted the bastards who killed Fahad to pay for killing him. He wanted the racists who stabbed him and left him for dead to pay for what they did, and not get away with it like they had.

He wanted to have a purpose beyond the ordinary. He wanted to stand for something. To be part of something grander.

He wanted his family to be proud of him. He wanted his father to love him, not for who they wanted him to be, but for who he was.

But, as he looked back at Sullivan, ignoring the shouts and the commotion and the terror, he wished he was as confident as this man was.

To have witnessed the horrors he'd witnessed and still be as calm and rational as he was.

"I—" Zain began to say.

"What?" Sullivan prompted. "What is it? What do you want?"

"I — I want to not be scared anymore. More than anything, I just don't want to be scared."

He was crying. He felt pathetic.

But Sullivan didn't treat him like he was pathetic.

He put his arm around Zain's back, pressed his head onto his shoulder, and hugged him.

Such a small gesture, one that we're taught isn't manly — but one that made all the difference.

"Right," Sullivan said. "Get the vest off, quickly."

Watching to see if the firearms had seen, Sullivan helped Zain lift his top off and undo the Velcro of his vest. Sullivan discarded it and its detonator on the ground, then Zain put his t-shirt back on.

"This way," Sullivan instructed, and they ran toward the firearms units.

"What are we doing?" Zain objected.

"We need to get past them to leave."

"But look at me — they'll shoot me just for being Muslim."

Sullivan looked Zain in the eyes, and said, "Trust me."

So Zain did.

They ran through the airport and, as they reached the firearms unit, one of the officers stopped them.

Another pointed their gun at Zain's head.

Zain closed his eyes. Flinched. Got ready for the bullet to fire through his brain.

But nothing happened.

The officer frisked him. They patted his legs, his chest, his arms, and then, when they were done, the officer turned back to his colleagues.

"He's clean," the officer said.

"Thank you," Zain said, though he wasn't sure why.

"Told you," Sullivan said, with a little grin, and they ran out, following the crowds.

Zain looked to either side of him as he did. There were families running, kids running, old people running — and Muslims running.

He looked at them, astounded that people were not fleeing from him or these other followers of Islam. They were all running to safety together.

"Target found!" he heard an officer shout.

They'd found the vest. Still running, Zain tensed, and looked at Sullivan, who just carried on walking.

Sullivan glanced over his shoulder and, just as he did, he was sure he saw someone.

Someone who made him pause.

The woman next to the bomb vest... The face was familiar...

Her eyes met his.

Could it be?

His heart raced even harder, just for a moment.

Then he realised he was seeing things.

He wished it could be true, but it was delusions of an ageing, tired mind.

He shook his head to himself.

Kelly is dead.

He wished she wasn't. He wished he could undo all the nasty things he'd said, but she was dead.

It was like when he saw Talia in his dreams. It was just wishful thinking, nothing more.

He turned, and he did not hesitate.
They carried on going, and left the airport.

CHAPTER SIXTY-NINE

Kelly had left the boot of the car to find Azeer Nadeem's corpse on the floor. There were two others who were dead, too, but this didn't look like the work of the firearms unit, there were no bullets in Azeer's body.

Which made her wonder...

Had Sullivan found a way?

She looked up. She was at Heathrow Airport.

Oh, God...

She panicked.

She entered the airport, greeted by a woman's voice telling people to evacuate. A mass of people ran toward her, racing toward the exits.

She ignored them, put her arms in front of her face, forced her way through the mass of bodies, and emerged into the terminal — people still pushed past her, but she was no longer surrounded. She looked around, at the empty coffee shop, at the empty money exchange counter, at the empty waiting area.

And then she saw him. Up a level, far into the distance.

Sullivan.

The firearms units were a few metres in front of her, searching for the attacker. She recognised the scared-looking boy standing opposite Sullivan as the man she'd seen praying with Azeer.

But Sullivan was not beating up this boy. In fact, it looked like they were talking.

This man, a former assassin who Kelly had been told was a cruel, cold-blooded monster, stood opposite a boy he could quite easily take down. He could get that detonator off the boy and stop this instantly.

But he didn't.

Why didn't he?

Then again — why hadn't the boy hit the detonator yet?

Then something remarkable happened.

Sullivan, whom Jameson had claimed was a ruthless murderer, put his hand on Zain's back, and pulled him in close.

They hugged.

Kelly wasn't sure Sullivan had ever hugged her, but he hugged this boy.

She felt herself crying.

Sullivan had done so much to resist her affection, to insist that he was not in love, to prove he was this blunt, uncaring man — yet here he was, proving her wrong.

He helped the boy remove his bullet proof vest, placing it on the floor along with the detonator.

And they ran.

They paused for the firearm's unit to frisk them, then they kept running.

She reached her arm out, unable to believe he was actually here.

"Jay..."

But he didn't see or hear her. He rushed straight past, preoccupied with getting the boy to safety.

She watched him disappear into the crowd. How could he not see her?

She wanted to go after him, but her job was her priority. She ran up the stairs and to the vest.

She waved her arms at the firearms.

"I'm from MI5, it's here!"

"Target found!" one of them shouted.

They ran to her, and radioed in the bomb squad. Their voices melded into the background as Kelly stared at the back of Sullivan's head.

Then, just as he was about to disappear out of sight, he looked back.

He saw her.

Their eyes met.

Finally, he saw her.

She held his gaze, willing him to come back to her, to be as happy to know she was still alive as she was to know he was okay.

She was about to run to him, about to leap into his arms, to kiss him, to listen to him apologise and tell her it would all be okay.

She'd tell him what she'd suffered for him, and he would thank her. He'd say he loved her. He'd say he was a fool.

But he didn't.

He looked away, then kept on running.

Despite looking at her, despite knowing she was okay, that she was still alive, he kept on running.

That was how much she meant to him.

The man she'd been tortured for did not even care that she was still alive.

Maybe he didn't love her after all. Maybe he'd actually meant everything he said.

"Goodbye," she said, so quietly only she could hear it.

She tried to stay and help, but the adrenaline soon ran out, and she collapsed from the pain and fatigue of the past few weeks.

She'd wake up in a hospital a few days later.

And she'd never see Sullivan again.

SOUTHEND, UNITED KINGDOM

THREE MONTHS LATER

CHAPTER SEVENTY

THEY HAD STAYED HIDDEN, AT FIRST.

After all, they were wanted men.

Sullivan watched the news reports on the television. They reported how he had escaped from prison, and was once again on the government's most-wanted list.

It was no different to how it had always been.

He was wanted by many governments and gangsters. There was always a price tag on his head. Soon, his face would stop being printed in newspapers, the media would move onto another story and he'd just keep moving from place to place as he always did.

As for Zain, they had to make sure no one was after him. Zain had walked through the airport, and he had dumped the vest, and CCTV would have caught his journey. The question was whether they had identified him.

They hid in Lisbon for a few months before returning to the United Kingdom; somewhere close enough to home that they could return quickly, but busy enough that they could disappear.

As it was, it didn't appear that they had identified Zain.

CCTV images were broadcast of him walking through Heathrow as the news reported on a foiled terrorist attack, but Zain rarely looked up. One of the benefits of the boy's lack of confidence was that he always looked to his feet. All they had was a video of a man they couldn't recognise.

The police appealed for help and seemed to become more and more desperate for a lead.

Still, Sullivan wasn't stupid — he knew they could be pretending not to know who Zain was to lull them into a false sense of security. They didn't take the risk.

Of course, one may wonder why Sullivan was protecting a potential terrorist and a former Alhami member. He could hand Zain over to the police, of course. They could charge him. Maybe even torture him, if they believed that he had more information. But he was just a kid, and he did not deserve to be persecuted for his anger. His path had been wayward, and he had stumbled into an awful situation, but it was not his fault.

It was a path this world had created for him.

More specifically, that this country had created for him.

If it hadn't been for a brutal act of racism when Zain was just sixteen years old, committed by products of prejudice buried deep within society, then he wouldn't have been so angry. It was a vicious cycle — they would kill Zain's friends, Zain would kill their friends, so they would kill Zain's friends and Zain would kill theirs and it would not stop.

Besides, if Sullivan had not witnessed an act of murder at sixteen years old, maybe he would not have started his own vicious cycle.

Different walks of life still followed the same path.

He smirked as he pulled off the motorway. He just invented his very own cliché. He wondered if it would catch on.

Eventually, Sullivan brought the car to a stop outside the

house Zain had put into the Sat Nav. Zain didn't get out, and they sat in the same silence they'd been in for the entire journey.

"You don't have to do this," Sullivan said.

"Nah, I got to do it sometime."

"We can wait."

"I have to face them. I have to, I just..."

Zain looked at his fidgeting hands.

"What if they don't accept me back?" he asked.

"They might not."

"You think?"

"If you hurt them so much, then they may be angry. Who knows?"

"So what do I do then? Just leave?"

"God, no. You stay."

Zain looked confused.

"Even if they are pissed off?"

"Especially if they are pissed off. Show them you mean business. If they give you a shitty time, then you admit you deserve it and have a shitty time."

"I just don't—"

"Hey — at least you still have a family."

Zain nodded.

He took a deep breath, readied himself, and opened the door.

Then he paused. Looked back at Sullivan.

"What about you?" he asked.

"What do you mean, what about me?"

"You got any family to go back to?"

"No. Besides, the whole country's hunting me. I'll find somewhere abroad to stay for a few months where no one cares. Somewhere I can disappear."

"Then what?"

Sullivan shrugged. "Who knows?"

Zain went to speak, then struggled over his words.

"How do I say thank you?" he asked.

"What?" Sullivan was a little startled.

"For what you've done."

"You can thank me by going in there and facing your family, you bloody idiot."

Zain smiled. He held out his hand for a handshake — not a formal one, but one where his arm lifted upwards.

Sullivan took it.

Zain winked.

Damn, this kid was slick.

He left the car. Closed the door. Nodded.

Sullivan watched as he walked down the path.

Zain paused. Looked at his feet, took a deep breath, and rang the bell.

The door opened.

A woman stood there. Staring at him.

They did nothing at first.

Then Zain spoke. Sullivan couldn't tell what he said, but the minute he finished, his mother burst into tears, crying with such anguish that it took her to her knees.

Zain went to his knees with her, placing his arms around her as she wept.

His father appeared.

Zain said something to him, something that looked like, "I'm so sorry."

His father didn't join the hug, but he put a hand on Zain's back.

They went inside the house and closed the door.

Sullivan was a little jealous. He'd lost everyone he'd ever loved. Whether it be his abusive parents, his loving wife, his daughter, or even Kelly.

Talia was still alive, but he had no idea where she was. Maybe they'd find each other again someday, who knows?

But at least Zain had avoided Sullivan's fate. At least he'd done that.

In twenty years' time, Zain would be living in his own home with kids and a wife. Not spending his time drinking in a bar like Sullivan.

But Sullivan couldn't wait around. He couldn't risk being seen. He had to leave.

So he drove on. Onto the motorway, to the airport, and to another country.

Maybe someday he'd have a daughter again. Maybe someday he'd have some resemblance of life. Or, maybe he'd learn to just be content with being alive.

Whatever happens, Zain had given him hope. This boy had overcome his anger, and was now free to have whatever life he wished to have.

Zain had been freed from his prison and, someday, maybe Sullivan hoped that he could be freed from his.

WOULD YOU LIKE A FREE BOOK?

Join Ed Grace's mailing list and get FREE and EXCLUSIVE novella that tells the story of how Jay Sullivan was recruited to be an assassin...

Join at www.edgraceauthor.com/sign-up

ED GRACE

A DEADLY WEAPON

A Jay Sullivan Thriller

ED GRACE

ASSASSIN DOWN

A Jay Sullivan Thriller

ED GRACE

KILL THEM QUICKLY

A Jay Sullivan Thriller

Printed in Great Britain
by Amazon

60011093R00203